NOVELS BY THOMAS MCGUANE

The Sporting Club   (*1969*)

The Bushwhacked Piano   (*1971*)

Ninety-Two in the Shade   (*1973*)

Panama   (*1978*)

PANAMA

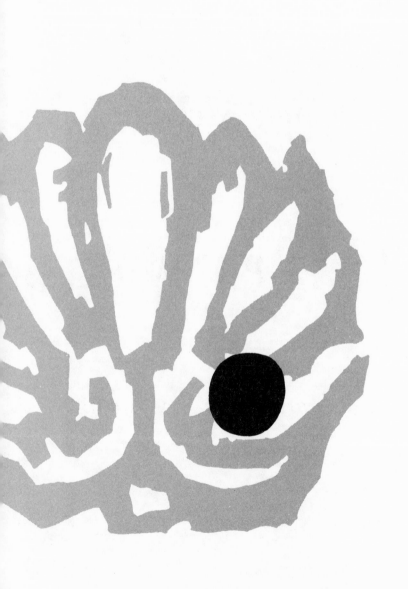

Thomas McGuane

PANAMA

Farrar, Straus and Giroux

NEW YORK

For Jim Harrison

———————

The best epitaph a man can gain is to have

accomplished daring deeds of valor against the

enmity of fiends during his lifetime.

THE SEAFARER

PANAMA

1

THIS IS THE FIRST TIME I've worked without a net. I want to tell the truth. At the same time, I don't want to start a feeding frenzy. You stick your neck out and you know what happens. It's obvious.

The newspaper said that the arrests were made by thirty agents in coordinated raids "early in the a.m." and that when the suspects were booked, a crowd of three hundred gathered at the Monroe County Courthouse and applauded. The rest of the page had to do with the charges against the men, which were neither here nor there. Most people I heard talking thought it was just too Cuban for words.

I stepped out onto the patio as the city commissioner was taken to the unmarked car in handcuffs.

He was in his bathrobe and lottery tickets were blowing all over the place. Last week they picked up my dog and it cost me a five. The phone number was on her collar and they could have called. I knew how badly they had wanted to use the gas. But then, they're tired of everything. The wind blows all winter and gets on your nerves. It just does. They have nothing but their uniforms and the hopes of using the gas.

Out on the patio, I could see the horizon. The dog slept in the wedge of sun. There were no boats, the sea was flat, and from here, there was not a bit of evidence of the coordinated raids, the unmarked cars. The lottery—the bolita—was silent; it was always silent. And behind the wooden shutters, there was as much cocaine as ever. I had a pile of scandal magazines to see what had hit friends and loved ones. There was not one boat between me and an unemphatic horizon. I was home from the field of agony or whatever you want to call it; I was home from it. I was dead.

I went up to the Casa Marina to see my stepmother. The cats were on the screen above the enclosed pool and the grapefruits were rotting in the little grove. Ruiz the gardener was crawfishing on the Cay Sal bank and the bent grass was thick and spongy and neglected. I was there five minutes when she said, "You were an overnight sensation." And I said, "Gotta hit it, I left the motor running." And she said, "You left the motor running?" and I said, "That's it for me, I'm going." And she tottered after me with the palmetto bugs scattering in the foyer and screamed at me as I pulled out: "You left the motor running! You don't have a car!" I actually don't know how smart she is. What could she have meant by that? I believe that she was attacking my memory.

She is a special case, Roxy; she is related to me three different ways and in some sense collects all that is dreary, sinister, or in any way glorious about my family. Roxy is one of those who have technically died; was in fact pronounced dead, then accidentally discovered still living by an alert nurse. She makes the most of this terrible event. She sometimes has need of tranquilizers half the size of Easter eggs. She drinks brandy and soda with them; and her face hollows out everywhere, her eyes sink, and you think of her earlier death. Sometimes she raises her hand to her face thinking the drink is in it. Roxy can behave with great charm. But then, just at the wrong time, pulls up her dress or throws something. I time my visits with extreme caution. I watch the house or see if her car has been properly parked. I used to spy but then I saw things which I perhaps never should have; and so I stopped that. When she thinks of me as an overnight sensation, she can be quite ruthless, flinging food at me or, without justification, calling the police and making false reports. I tolerate that because, under certain circumstances, I myself will stop at nothing. Fundamentally though, my stepmother is a problem because she is disgusting.

I guess it came to me, or maybe I just knew, that I have not been remembering things as clearly as I could have. For instance, Roxy is right, I don't have a car. I have a memory problem. The first question—look, you can ask me this—is exactly how much evasive editing is part of my loss of memory. I've been up against that one before. My position with respect to anyone else's claims for actuality has always been: it's you against me and may the best man win.

I'm not as stupid as I look. Are you? For instance, I'm no golfer. I did have a burst, and this is the ghastly thing which awaits each of us, of creating the world in my own image. I removed all resistance until I floated in my own invention. I creamed the opposition. Who in the history of ideas has prepared us for creaming the opposition? This has to be understood because otherwise . . . well, there is no otherwise; it really doesn't matter.

The first time I ran into Catherine, coming from the new wing of the county library, I watched from across the street noting that her Rhonda Fleming, shall we say, *grandeur* had not diminished. It seemed a little early in the present voyage to reveal myself. I sat on the wall under the beauty parlor, just a tenant in my self, or a bystander, eyes flooded, pushing my fingers into my sleeves like a nun. I thought, *When I find the right crooked doctor, I'm going to laugh in your face.*

I followed her for two blocks and watched her turn up the blind lane off Caroline where the sapodilla tree towers up from the interior of the block as though a piece of the original forest were imprisoned there. This spring they dug up the parking lot behind some clip joint on lower Duval and found an Indian grave, the huge skull of a Calusa seagoing Indian staring up through four inches of blacktop at the whores, junkies, and Southern lawyers.

So I sent her flowers without a note and two days later a note without flowers; and got this in return, addressed "Chester Hunnicutt Pomeroy, General Delivery": "Yes Chet I know you're home. But don't call me now, you flop you. —Catherine." I went into the garden and opened the toolshed, bug life running out among the rake tines. I got the big English stainless-steel pruning shears and came, you take it from me, *that* close to sending Catherine the finger I'd lost in her darkness so many thousands of times. The palmetto bugs are translucent as spar varnish and run over your feet in the shed. The sea has hollowed the patio into resonant chambers and when the wind has piped up like today you hear its moiling, even standing in the shed with the rakes and rust and bugs.

I felt better and lost all interest in mutilating myself, even for Catherine. Tobacco doves settled in the crown-of-thorns and some remote airplane changed harmonics overhead with a soft pop like champagne, leaving a pure white seam on the sky. I was feeling better and better and better. On stationery from my uncle's shipyard, I wrote, "There is no call for that. I'm just here with respect of healing certain injuries. Catherine, you only hurt hurt hurt when you lash out like that. I don't believe you try to picture what harm you do. —Chet." I traced my finger on the back of the sheet with a dotted line where the shears would have gone through. I said nothing as to the dotted line. It seemed to me with some embarrassment that it might have looked like a request for a ring.

I dialed Information and asked for Catherine Clay. The operator said it was unpublished. I told her it was a matter of life or death; and the operator said, I know who you are, and clicked off. They wouldn't treat Jesse James like that.

When they build a shopping center over an old salt marsh, the seabirds sometimes circle the same place for a year or more, coming back to check daily, to see if there isn't some little chance those department stores and pharmacies and cinemas won't go as quickly as they'd come. Similarly, I come back and keep looking into myself, and it's always steel, concrete, fan magazines, machinery, bubble gum; nothing as sweet as the original marsh. Catherine knows this without looking, knows that the loving child who seems lost behind the reflector Ray-Bans, perhaps or probably really is lost. And the teeth that were broken in schoolyards or spoiled with Cuban ice cream have been resurrected and I am in all respects the replica of an effective bright-mouthed coastal omnivore, as happy with spinach salads as human flesh; and who snoozing in the sun of his patio, inert as any rummy, Rolex Oyster Chronometer imbedding slightly in softened flesh, teeth glittering with ocean light like minerals, could be dead; could be the kind of corpse that is sometimes described as "fresh."

"I am a congestion of storage batteries. I'm wired in series. I've left some fundamental com-

ponents on the beach, and await recharging, bom-
bardment, implanting, *something*, shall we say, very
close to the bone. I do want to go on; but having
given up, I can't be expected to be very sympathetic."

"That's all very pretty," Catherine Clay said.
"But I don't care. Now may I go?"

"There's more."

"I don't care. And above all, I don't want you
stalking me like this in the supermarket. I can't have
you lurking in the aisles."

"It's still the same."

"It's not, you liar, you flop!"

Slapping me, crying, yelling, oh God, clerks
peering. I said, "You're prettiest like this." She
chunks a good one into my jaw. The groceries were
on the floor. Someone was saying, "Ma'am? Ma'am?"
My tortoiseshell glasses from Optique Boutique were
askew and some blood was in evidence. My lust for
escape was complete. Palm fronds beat against the
air-conditioned thermopane windows like my own
hands.

Two clerks were helping Catherine to the door.
I think they knew. Mrs. Fernandez, the store manager, stood by me.

"Can I use the crapper?" I asked.

She stared at me coolly and said, "First aisle
past poultry."

I stood on the toilet and looked out at my nation
through the ventilator fan. Any minute now, and
Catherine Clay, the beautiful South Carolina wild
child, would appear shortcutting her way home with
her groceries.

I heard her before I could see her. She wasn't

breathing right. That scene in the aisles had been too much for her and her esophagus was constricted. She came into my view and in a very deep and penetrating voice I told her that I still loved her, terrifying myself that it might not be a sham, that quite apart from my ability to abandon myself to any given moment, I might in fact still be in love with this crafty, amazing woman who looked up in astonishment. I let her catch no more than a glimpse of me in the ventilator hole before pulling the bead chain so that I vanished behind the dusty accelerating blades, a very effective slow dissolve.

I put my sunglasses back on and stood in front of the sink, staring at my blank reflection, scrutinizing it futilely for any expression at all and committing self-abuse. The sunglasses looked silvery and pure in the mirror, showing twins of me, and I watched them until everything was silvery and I turned off the fan, tidied up with a paper towel, and went back out through poultry toward the electric doors. Mrs. Fernandez, the store manager, smiled weakly and I said, "Bigger even than I had feared." The heat hit me in the street and I started . . . I think I started home. It was to feed the dog but I was thinking of Catherine and I had heartaches by the million.

My father was a store detective who was killed in the Boston subway fire, having gone to that city in connection with the Bicentennial. He had just left Boston Common, where we have kin buried. Everything I say about my father is disputed by everyone. My family have been shipwrights and ship's chandlers, except for him and me. I have been as you know in the Svengali business; I saw a few things and raved for money. I had a very successful show called *The Dog Ate The Part We Didn't Like*. I have from time to time scared myself. Even at the height of my powers, I was not in good health. But a furious metabolism preserves my physique and I am considered a tribute to evil living.

Those who have cared for me, friends, uncles, lovers, think I'm a lost soul or a lost cause. When I'm tired and harmless, I pack a gun, a five-shot Smith and Wesson .38. It's the only .38 not in a six-shot configuration I know of. How the sacrifice of that one last shot makes the gun so flat and concealable, so deadlier than the others. Just by giving up a little!

As to my mother, she was a flash act of the early fifties, a bankrolled B-girl who caught cancer like a bug that was going around; and died at fifty-six pounds. There you have it. The long and the short of it. And I had a brother Jim.

The money began in a modest way in the 1840's. A grandfather of minor social bearing, who had fought a successful duel, married a beautiful girl from the Canary Islands with two brothers who were ship's carpenters. They built coasters, trading smacks, sharpie mailboats, and a pioneer lightship for the St. Lucie inlet. The Civil War came and they built two blockade runners for the rebellion, the *Red Dog* and the *Rattlesnake*; went broke, jumped the line to Key West again while Stephen Mallory left town to become Secretary of the Confederate Navy. At what is now the foot of Ann Street, they built a series of deadly blockade boats, light, fast, and armed. They were rich by then, had houses with pecan wood dining-room tables, crazy chandeliers, and dogwood joists pinned like the ribs of ships. Soon they were all dead; but the next gang were solid and functional and some of them I remember. Before our shipyard went broke in the Depression, they had built every kind of seagoing conveyance that could run to Cuba and home; the prettiest, a turtle schooner, the *Hillary B. Cates*, was seen last winter off Cap Haitien with a black crew, no masts, and a tractor engine for power, afloat for a century. She had been a yacht and a blockade runner, and her first master, a child Confederate officer from the Virginia Military Institute, was stabbed to death by her engineer, Noah Card, who defected to the North and raised oranges at Zephyrhills, Florida, until 1931. He owed my grandfather money; but I forget why.

My grandfather was a dull, stupid drunk; and the white oak and cedar and longleaf pine rotted and the floor fell out of the mold loft while he filed patents on automobiles and comic cigarette utensils. I recall only his rheumy stupor and his routine adoration of children.

Let me try Catherine again.

"One more and I go to the police for a restraining order."

No sense pursuing that for the moment.

My stepmother had a suitor. He was an attorney-at-law and affected argyle socks and low blue automobiles. He screamed when he laughed. What I think he knew was that the shipyard was a world of waterfront property and that when the Holiday Inn moved in where the blockade boats and coasters had been built, Roxy got all the money. His name was Curtis Peavey and he was on her case like a man possessed, running at the house morning noon and night with clouds of cheap flowers. Roxy had been known to fuck anything; and I couldn't say she ever so much as formed an opinion of Peavey. I noticed though that she didn't *throw* the flowers away, she pushed them into the trash, blossoms forward, as if they'd been involved in an accident. In this, I pretended to see disgust. I myself didn't like Peavey. His eyes were full of clocks, machinery, and numbers. The curly head of hair tightened around his scalp when he talked to me and his lips stuck on his teeth. But he had a devoted practice. He represented Catherine. No sense concealing that. If Peavey could, he'd throw the book at me. He said I was depraved and licentious; he said that to Roxy. Whenever I saw him, he was always about to motivate in one of the low blue cars. Certain people thought of him as a higher type; he donated Sandburg's life of Lincoln to the county library with his cornball bookplate in every volume, a horrific woodcut of a sturdy New England tree; with those dismal words: Curtis G. Peavey. As disgusting as Roxy was, I didn't like to see her gypped; which is what Peavey clearly meant to do. I didn't care about the money at all. I have put that shipyard up my nose ten times over.

.

I don't think Peavey was glad to see me hunker next to him on the red stool. The fanaticism with which he slurped down the bargain quantities of ropa vieja, black beans, and yellow rice suggested a speedy exit.

I said, "Hello, Curtis."

"How long are you back for—"

"Got a bit of it on your chin there, didn't you."

"Here, yes, pass me one of those."

"How's Roxy holding up?" I asked.

"She's more than holding up. A regular iron woman."

"A regular what?"

"Iron woman."

"You want another napkin?"

"Get out of here you depraved pervert."

I said, "You'll never get her money."

"I'd teach you a lesson," said Curtis Peavey, rising to his feet and deftly thumbing acrylic pleats from his belt line, "but you're carrying a gun, aren't you?"

"Yes," I said, "to perforate your duodenum."

"You have threatened me," he said softly. "Did you hear that, shit-for-brains? It won't do." Peavey strolled into the heat and wind. I stopped at the cash register and paid for his slop.

I went for a walk.

Something started the night I rode the six-hundred-pound Yorkshire hog into the Oakland auditorium; I was double-billed with four screaming soul monsters and I shut everything down as though I'd burned the building. I had dressed myself in Revolutionary War throwaways and a top hat, much

like an Iroquois going to Washington to ask the
Great White Father to stop sautéing his babies.
When they came over the lights, I pulled a dagger
they knew I'd use. I had still not replaced my upper
front teeth and I helplessly drooled. I was a hundred
and eighty-five pounds of strangely articulate shriek-
ing misfit and I would go too god damn far.

At the foot of Seminary I stopped to look at a
Czech marine diesel being lowered into a homemade
trap boat on a chain fall. It was stolen from Cuban
nationals, who get nice engines from the Reds. The
police four-wheel drifted around the corner aiming
riot guns my way. Getting decency these days is like
pulling teeth. Once the car was under control and
stopped, two familiar officers, Nylon Pinder and
Platt, put me up against the work shed for search.

"Drive much?" I asked.

"Alla damn time," said Platt.

"Why work for Peavey?" I asked.

Platt said, "He's a pillar of our society. When
are you gonna learn the ropes?"

Nylon Pinder said, "He don't have the gun on
him."

Platt wanted to know, "What you want with the
.38 Smith?"

"It's for Peavey's brain pan. I want him to see
the light. He's a bad man."

"Never register a gun you mean to use. Get a
cold piece. Peavey's a pillar of our society."

"Platt said that."

"Shut up, you. He's a pillar of our society and
you're a depraved pervert."

"Peavey said that."

"Nylon said for you to shut your hole, misfit."

"I said that, I said 'misfit.' "

Platt did something sudden to my face. There was blood. I pulled out my bridge so if I got trounced I wouldn't swallow it. Platt said, "Look at that, will you."

I worked my way around the Czech diesel. They were going to leave me alone now. "Platt," I said, "when you off?"

"Saturdays. You can find me at Rest Beach."

"Depraved pervert," said Nylon, moving only his lips in that vast face. "Get some teeth," he said. "You look like an asshole."

The two of them sauntered away. I toyed with the notion of filling their mouths with a couple of handfuls of bees, splitting their noses, pushing small live barracudas up their asses. The mechanic on the chain fall said, "What did they want with you? Your nose is bleeding."

"I'm notorious," I said. "I'm cheating society and many of my teeth are gone. Five minutes ago I was young. You saw me! What is this? I've given my all and this is the thanks I get. If Jesse James had been here, he wouldn't have let them do that."

The mechanic stared at me and said, "*Right.*"

I hiked to my stepmother's, to Roxy's. I stood like a druid in her doorway and refused to enter. "You and your Peavey," I said. "I can't touch my face."

"Throbs?"

"You and your god damn Peavey."

"He won't see me any more. He says you've

made it impossible. I ought to kill you. But your father will be here soon and he'll straighten you out."

"Peavey buckled, did he? I don't believe that. He'll be back. —And my father is dead."

"Won't see me any more. Peavey meant something and now he's gone. He called me his tulip."

"His . . . ?"

"You heard me."

I gazed at Roxy. She looked like a circus performer who had been shot from the cannon one too many times.

In family arguments, things are said which are so heated and so immediate as to seem injuries which could never last; but which in fact are never forgotten. Now nothing is left of my family except two uncles and this tattered stepmother who technically died; nevertheless, I can trace myself through her to those ghosts, those soaring, idiot forebears with their accusations, and their steady signal that, whatever I thought I was, I was not the real thing. We had all said terrible things to each other, added insult to injury. My father had very carefully taken me apart and thrown the pieces away. And now his representatives expected me to acknowledge his continued existence.

So, you might ask, why have anything to do with Roxy? I don't know. It could be that after the anonymity of my fields of glory, coming back had to be something better than a lot of numinous locations, the house, the convent school, Catherine. Maybe not Catherine. Apart from my own compulsions, which have applied to as little as the open road, I don't know what she has to do with the price of beans . . . I thought I'd try it anyway. Catherine. Roxy looked inside me.

"Well, you be a good boy and butt out. Somehow, occupy yourself. We can't endlessly excuse you because you're recuperating. I *died* and got less attention. Then, I was never an overnight sensation."

I went home and fed the dog, this loving speckled friend who after seven trying years in my life has never been named. The dog. She eats very little and stares at the waves. She kills a lizard; then, overcome with remorse, tips over in the palm shadows for a troubled snooze.

Catherine stuck it out for a while. She stayed with me at the Sherry-Netherland and was in the audience when I crawled out of the ass of a frozen elephant and fought a duel in my underwear with a baseball batting practice machine. She looked after my wounds. She didn't quit until late. There was no third party in question.

I could throw a portion of my body under a passing automobile in front of Catherine's house. A rescue would be necessary. Catherine running toward me resting on my elbows, my crushed legs on the pavement between us. All is forgiven. I'll be okay. I'll learn to remember. We'll be happy together.

I had a small sharpie sailboat which I built with my own hands in an earlier life and which I kept behind the A&B Lobster House next to the old cable schooner. I did a handsome job on this boat if I do say so; and she has survived both my intermediate career and neglect. I put her together like a fiddle, with longleaf pine and white-oak frames, fastened with bronze. She has a rabbeted chine and I let the centerboard trunk directly into the keel, which was tapered at both ends. Cutting those changing bevels in hard pine and oak took enormous concentration and drugs; not the least problem was in knowing ahead of time that it would be handy to have something I had made still floating when my life fell apart years later.

She had no engine and I had to row her in and out of the basin. When the wind dropped, I'd just let the canvas slat around while I hung over the transom staring down the light shafts into the depths. Then when it piped up, she'd trim herself and I'd slip around to the tiller and take things in hand. Sailboats were never used in the Missouri border fighting.

I went out today because my nose hurt from Peavey's goons and because I was up against my collapse; and because Catherine wouldn't see me. My hopes were that the last was the pain of vanity. It would be reassuring to think that my ego was sufficiently intact as to sustain injury; but I couldn't bank that yet.

The wind was coming right out of the southeast fresh, maybe eight or ten knots, and I rowed just clear of the jetty and ran up the sails, cleated off the jib, sat back next to the tiller, pointed her up as good as I could, and jammed it right in close to the shrimp boats before I came about and tacked out of the basin. I stayed on that tack until I passed two iron wrecks and came about again. The sharpie is so shoal I could take off cross-country toward the Bay Keys without fear of going aground. I trimmed her with the sail, hands off the tiller, cleated the main sheet, and turned on some Cuban radio. I put my feet up and went half asleep and let the faces parade past.

Immediately east of the Pearl Basin, I found a couple shivering on a sailboard they had rented at the beach. He was wearing a football jersey over long nylon surfing trunks; and she wore a homemade bikini knotted on her brown, rectilineal hips. What healthy people! They had formed a couple and rented a sailboard. They had clean shy smiles, and though they may not have known their asses from a hole in the ground in terms of a personal philosophy, they seemed better off for it, happier, even readier for life and death than me with my ceremonious hours of thought and unparalleled acceleration of experience.

I rigged the board so that it could be sailed again, standing expertly to the lee of them with my sail luffing. I told them they were ready to continue their voyage and she said to the boy, "Hal, it's a bummer, I'm freezing." And Hal asked me if she could ride back in my boat because it was drier. I told them I'd be sailing for a while, that I had come out to think, that I was bad company, and that my father had died in the subways of Boston. They said that was okay, that she would be quiet and not bother me. I let her come aboard, politely concealing my disappointment; then shoved Hal off astern. He was soon underway, with his plastic sailboard spanking on the chop, the bright cigarette advertisement on his sail rippling against the blue sky.

I continued toward the Bay Keys while the girl watched me with cold gray eyes, the shadow of the sail crossing her slowly at each tack. Then she went forward and took the sun with her hands behind her head.

"Your boyfriend a football player?" I asked.

"No, he deals coke."

"I see."

"Do you like coke?"

"Yes, quite a lot."

"Well, Hal has some Bolivian rock you can read your fortune in, I'll tell you that."

"Oh, gee, I—"

"Anybody ever tell you the difference between acid and coke?"

"Nobody ever did."

"Well, with acid you think you see God. With coke you think you *are* God. I'll tell you the honest truth, this rock Hal's got looks like the main exhibit at the Arizona Rock and Gem Show. Did you ever hear a drawl like mine?"

"No, where's it from?"

"It's not from anywhere. I made the god damn thing up out of magazines."

"How much of that rock is left?"

"One o.z. No more, no less. At a grand, it's the last nickel bargain in Florida."

"I'll take it all."

"We'll drop it off. Hey, can you tell me one thing, how come you got hospitalized? The papers

said exhaustion but I don't believe everything I read.
You don't look exhausted."

"It was exhaustion."

That night, after I had paid them, I asked if the
business in the boats that afternoon had been a
setup. She said that it had. "Don't tell him that!"
giggled the boyfriend. "You coo-coo brain!"

My eyes were out on wires and I was grind-
ing my teeth. When I chopped that shit, it fell apart
like a dog biscuit. Bolivian rock. I didn't care. I just
made the rails about eight feet and blew myself a
daydream with a McDonald's straw. Let them try
and stop me now!

By the time I got to Reynolds Street I was in
tears. I went down to the park and crossed over to
Astro City. The ground was beaten gray and flat and
the tin rocketships were unoccupied. I climbed high
enough on the monkey bars that no one could look
into my eyes and wept until I choked.

I considered changing my name and cutting my
throat. I considered taking measures. I decided to
walk to Catherine's house again and if necessary nail
myself to her door. I was up for the whole shooting
match.

I walked over to Simonton, past the old cigar
factory, around the schoolyard and synagogue, and
stopped at the lumber company. I bought a hammer and four nails. Then I continued on my way. On
Eaton Street, trying to sneak, I dropped about a
gram on the sidewalk. I knelt with my red and white
straw and snorted it off the concrete while horrified

pedestrians filed around me. *"It takes toot to tango,"* I explained. Nylon and Platt would love to catch me at this, a real chance to throw the book. I walked on, rubbing a little freeze on my gums and waiting for the drip to start down my throat and signal the advent of white-line fever or renewed confidence.

The wind floated gently into my hair, full of the ocean and maritime sundries from the shipyard. A seagull rocketed all the way from William Street close to the wooden houses, unseen, mind you, by any eyes but mine. A huge old tamarind dropped scented moisture into the evening in trailing veils. Mad fuck-ups running to their newspapers and greasy dinners surged around my cut-rate beneficence. I felt my angel wings unfold. More than that you can't ask for.

Catherine's house with her bicycle on the porch was in a row of wooden cigarmakers' houses grown about with untended vegetation, on a street full of huge mahoganies. I thought to offer her a number of things—silence, love, friendship, departure, a hot beef injection, shining secrets, a tit for a tat, courtesy, a sensible house pet, a raison d'être, or a cup of coffee. And I was open to suggestion, short of "get outa here," in which case I had the hammer and nails and would nail myself to her door like a summons.

I crossed the street to her house, crept Indian style onto the porch, and looked through the front window. Catherine was asleep on the couch in her shorts and I thought my heart would stop. I studied her from this luxurious point, staring at the wildly curly hair on her bare back; her arm hung down and her fingertips just rested on the floor next to a crammed ashtray. I had the nails in my shirt pocket, the hammer in the top of my pants like Jesse James's Colt.

"Catherine," I said, "you let me in." This handsome woman, whom Peavey had once had the nerve to call my common-law wife, was suddenly on her feet, walking toward me with jiggling breasts, to ram down the front window and bolt the door. Then she went upstairs and out of sight. I called her name a couple of more times, got no answer, and nailed my left hand to the door with Jesse's Colt.

2

THE SILVER ROOFS extended from my window in a fractured line under a sky which displayed a small but ineffably shiny cloud to the west. The radio was playing "Volare" by Dean Martin, the notorious companion of Frank Sinatra.

Catherine, bless her heart maybe, Catherine pried me from the door and put me in the guest room. Then she had Doctor Proctor come over and load me good on some intravenous downer. At first I thought I had passed into the great beyond. I thought quite objectively about the dead. They are given so much credit; when, in fact, they don't know much of anything. And why should they? They have enough to do.

I'm busy too. I'm still alive and I'm not ashamed

of it. I'm proud of this raiment. Bring on the ghosts. I'll pack them through the streets. Let the ones who have ringed the city, who have made our lives an encampment, let them whiten the air, the sea. I happen to have enough to do already. Let the dead run a grocery store or build an airplane. I am not impressed with them, with the possible exception of my brother Jim. And having to argue as to whether my father is actually dead deprives the whole question of its dignity.

In the photograph of my mother's funeral party, I am the third mourner from the left. I am wearing a Countess Mara tie, older than me, whose blue flowers arise like ghosts toward my throat. It is widely presumed that the expression on my face is a raffish grin; whereas it is plainly the grimace of gastric distress.

In the foreground of the picture, my aunts carry on their bulbous flirtation with the photographer. The picture is covered with the somnolent stains of handling by interested parties who believed me to have been grinning.

By noontime, Catherine had not come home and I had suffered a whiteout, a silence, a space between the echoes of the dead I had trifled with; and I felt prefigured in the vacancy, as though my future inhered there.

My hand was bandaged, I had evidently passed out and hung from the nail until discovered. The muscles in my arm were sore and stretched. From dangling.

I was falling asleep again when I heard Catherine arrive with someone, unloading groceries in front. Then she and the other person, another young woman, came and sat on the bed and looked at me. I pretended to be asleep.

"He's still out of it," said the other woman.

"This is Marcelline," said Catherine.

"How did you know I was awake?"

"I can read you like a Dell comic."

"How do you do, Marcelline."

"Marcelline has just had an abortion."

"I wasn't making a pass at her, Catherine."

Marcelline said, "If I roll a J will you all smoke on it with me?" I told her that stuff was cluttering up the drug scene and that I was opposed to its use.

"Who gave you the abortion?" I asked. All I wanted was to talk to Catherine.

"A laughing nurse in New Orleans. A real card. I had to change planes in Tampa."

"Marcelline loves Tampa," Catherine said.

"They make a nice cigar there," I offered.

"How's your hand?"

"Hurts a lot."

"You had a nail in it," said Catherine.

Marcelline said, "A little crucifixion. What a droll guy. I hear you can't remember anything. You're full of little tricks."

"Used to be he just talked funny," said Catherine, "now he's commenced acting it out."

Marcelline said, "Tampa is full of elderly nice persons who know they could eat it any minute. So they don't talk nuts to get laughs. My, it hurts. That nurse just got in there and *rambled*."

I looked at Catherine with her berserk mass of kinks and curls. I thought, it didn't matter about men; but when push came to shove, these Southern girls only wanted to see each other. I didn't know what I was, not a Southerner certainly. A Floridian. Drugs, alligators, macadam, the sea, sticky sex, laughter, and sudden death. Catherine initiated the idea that I was a misfit. I took to the idea like a duck to water.

I felt sleepy again. I heard a sprinkler start up, the first drops of water falling on the ground with distinct thuds. I heard the voice of my odious grandfather twenty years ago, "There's a nigger fishing the canal and he's got one on!" My hands were knit together and I was wonderfully happy and comfortable drifting away with the two pretty women chatting on the end of the bed, about Tampa, about the difficulty of getting nice cotton things any more, about Wallace Stevens in Key West.

When I woke up a few minutes later, Marcelline was kissing Catherine. One of Catherine's little breasts was outside her shirt and her panties were stretched between her knees. Marcelline slid the green skirt over Catherine's stomach and bottom, then put it up under her. Catherine lifted one leg free of the panties in a gesture that put her leg out of the shadow the bed was in, into the sunlight. Marcelline slipped away and stayed until I heard the familiar tremolo of Catherine.

When Marcelline stood up, tucking a yellow forties washdress around her good Cajun body, she laughed suddenly. "He's awake!" Then leaned over and pinched my cheek. "I bet he jerked off the whole while!"

When Marcelline left, I said, "So that's it, eating pussy all day."

"Oh, God," she said, getting up. "I'm going to the beach. And when your hand is better, you're leaving too."

"Why did you take me in?"

"I was embarrassed to have you nailed on the door."

"Oh, Catherine. —Why am I itching?"

"My apartment's got a cistern under it and the mosquitoes are coming up through the floor."

"Have you turned queer?"

"Don't talk to me like that, you."

"Can I read my old love letters?"

"Burned them."

"Burned them! They're worth a fortune."

"To who? Other depraved perverts?"

"I just don't like that phrase. It's not a clever phrase. It's a dreary phrase and everybody's calling me it. I'm sick of it. You hurt with those hand-me-down phrases. They suggest indifference. Will you get in here with me?"

"No."

"You committed a crime against nature with Marcelline. What's wrong with me?"

"That's not the point, my dear. You'll forget we did."

"What's Marcelline do?"

"She's blackmailing a judge in Toronto."

"I still love you."

"Fuck off."

"With my whole heart."

"Why did you tell the magazines you regretted every minute with me?"

"Because you'd hurt me by disappearing without explanation, by leaving me flat. You can't do that to a psychotic."

"You told them that I was a nouveau Hitler maiden. Why?"

"Oh, did I do that?"

"That's why I call you a depraved pervert."

"Slip in here with me."

"No, I'm a big bull dike. I only like eating pussy. You called me deep-dish Southern plastic in a national publication."

"Catherine, don't ridicule me. I suspect your motives, doing that at the foot of my bed anyway."

"Come on, Chet, be the fun guy we knew you to be."

"Eat it."

"Not if it's a shlong."

"God, Catherine, I can't have this smut."

"Tell it to the dead elephant. Tell it to the creeps who said you're God. Tell it to the mayor of New York."

I stared at her, loving her hauteur, admiring that she was probably not going to buy it ever again. I wanted her. I was not down on sex, though some of my youthful flamboyance was no longer there.

She went to the wicker dresser and started raking idly through costume jewelry in a tray. She held the pretty junk to the light for an instant. Then her hands disappeared and her skirt fell. She turned and pulled the blouse over her head, then the little turned-in-knee two-step to get rid of the panties. She said, "Apologize."

"I'm sorry. Forgive me."

She slipped in beside me, skin cooler than mine, like an otter. I reached down. "What's that?"

"Marcelline."

"Gee. It's all over the place." I was a little disoriented, an orphan in the storm. I didn't know if I was what Catherine required. I really was not sure; but when I glided around, slipping all around and touching her, opening her in the slow rude way I remembered her liking, she was right there climbing up under it, thrilled. I loved her quite unselfishly, watching her all the time. She came in a languorous flood and called me Marcelline.

"I'll tell you what," she said—and by this time, she's walking around slamming drawers and assembling her duds to get the hell out, having behaved, by her lights, deplorably, having whipped it out—"you've gotten to where people can't even talk to you."

"What!"

"They know they're gonna get hustled and left high and dry while you cruise into this five-and-dime sunset."

"Oh, Catherine."

"It's true."

"I know it's true. But catch me when there are a few things I don't regret, would you?"

"I don't know what that means."

"Catch me when there's something I'm proud of. At the moment, I feel shit out of luck. I have some questions—"

"Shut up! Shut up shut up shut up!"

Items in the air. Why throw things now? I must be completely safe. I detest being injured.

"I can go. My hand's not that sore."

"I won't have your hand on my conscience! Now I'm feeling guilty! Can you beat that? Oh God, I want a restraining order!"

I got out of bed and snatched on my trousers. Boy oh boy was I in love. I started racing around for my belongings, trying to act like a cowboy but knowing full well what a duck I appeared. Something or other ricocheted from my head into the bathroom. A wooden coat hanger, I think it was. From the Sherry-Netherland. I was at Southard and Simonton before I knew it. There was a terrible squabble behind the wall opposite the police station. When I looked, I saw an older gentleman of the Cuban persuasion flogging an osprey out of his fighting cock runs. He had a gun.

Something about our republic makes us go armed. I myself am happier having a piece within reach, knowing if some goblin jumps into the path, it's away with him. Here in Key West, we take our guns to parties. My pedal steel player had one on a clip under his instrument; it said "Death To Traitors" on the backstrap and was stolen by a fan in Muscle Shoals, Alabama, on New Year's Day.

Why won't Catherine even try to see eye to eye with me about our future? I could see I stood a really good chance of not getting her back. I wonder if she actually has any right to make me feel this way. God, I want her back.

Back at my place, the ocean made a simpering

reedy wash under the eroded patio and my dog remembered my having failed to feed her last night.
Mrs. Dean, who lived next door and who weighed
much too much, felt her way across the crushed
coral to the ponderosa lemon tree and laid on it with
a flit gun until nothing could live there. I rattled
nourishing kibble into a tin plate and felt my nail
hole while the dog ate. My homecomings are always
this heartwarming, full of the familiars of our day-to-
day life, like radium watch dials, particle board,
novelty pills, or dental floss.

Catherine's yielding deprived me of a half-fore-
seen rape, something aesthetic to me, stooping over
her sunken form, pre-owned gabardine trousers
stretched across the piquant tendons behind my
knees. And her flippancy of course left me nothing in
terms of leverage, the way careless love leaves you
empty-handed. No tug, no give and take. Where
were the good old days?

I decided to throw a party, something nice,
something with an orchestra, by the sea with food,
the tradewinds in the sea grapes, the movements of
ocean at least as loud as the baseball or the drunks
on White Street. I would bring my dog and wind her
chain around the forearm of my linen jacket. I would
lean this way and that among the guests and say any
god damn thing I pleased because it was my fucking
party. I would order the guests about as whim provided. The servants would be little hippies with their
hair tied back and clean shirts. They will have left
the literature of revolutionary consciousness behind
in their pads. They would be made to hop to on the
highballs and party snacks. I would tell them

Krishna is the sound of petits fours in the teeth, the little shitsuckers.

By the time I had fed the dog, my two uncles, Pat and Jack, were in the patio. Pat used to throw the ball for my dead brother Jim and me up onto the amazing bevels of my father's roof and we would run around guessing wildly which way the ball would come down. Pat had all the time in the world for us, no matter that he was shell-shocked and having a time of it with his flagging law practice. Pat had a houseful of books, good cooking utensils, and a telescope in his attic. The rest of the family disapproved of him because he was a drunken queer.

Jack had all the family attention because he was a shipwright and kept the light of history burning. No one was building ships in Key West any more; but that didn't matter. We were all proud of him for whiling away his life in the shipyard, listening to bubble-gum music on AM radio, flipping his pocket-knife into the wall; and each year turning over the woodpile, catching the scorpions, and varnishing them on a piece of plywood over his desk. All Pat's years of struggling in his law office with his twitching shell-shocked face would never really supplant his behaving like a terrible fruit fly. When I was ten, my father ordered Pat to stay away from Jim and me.

Jack said, "Some place you got here."

"Just a seaside bide-a-wee."

Pat found the old tiles in the walls, old Havana

tiles with maidens and tobacco leaves blasted into the porcelain and no socialist realism in sight.

"Really quite a little place," Jack said.

"Are you retired or something?" Pat inquired.

Jack said, "Where's all your money? This place is okay for the dog. You were on Johnny Carson. Where's the simoleons, kiddo. This is no way to live."

"God," said Pat, "they could never make tiles like that again."

"It's in a numbered Swiss account," I said. "That way I could forget the number. It gives me humility, and humility is what I could stand a little of."

"You can say that again," said Jack.

Pat said, "I like everything you've done." Pat was the one who threw the ball over and over again for Jim and me.

"I'm having a party at the Casa Marina."

"The Casa Marina is abandoned. Besides, why don't you hold off for a while. Your father's supposed to be down soon on his boat."

"My father's dead," I said.

"That's a good one," said Jack.

"I know what he means," said Pat.

"There will be an orchestra and dancing in the weeds. Moonlight and whores in the old manner. Fireflies, bullbats, and phantom ships." I wanted to focus on the party.

"C'mon," Jack said. "We're just your uncles. We don't pay you to talk like that. They do."

Jack had me there. Here at home I wasn't being paid to sum up civilization or to act it out in a glimmer. Once again, I was Joe Blow and I wasn't sure I was crazy about it.

"The main thing," Jack said, "and I think Pat will agree. Whyn't you go on and stay the hell out of Roxy's business. She doesn't like it to start with. And also, we aren't situated on this island like we once were. Peavey could make it nasty. He's connected every which way and some of it's not too savory."

"He's dangerous," Pat said.

"I'll invite him to the party," I said.

"Come on, Chet."

"Yeah Chet gee."

I let some quiet fall and added, "Otherwise I'd, have to go ahead and shoot him."

"Don't even talk like that!"

"It doesn't matter anyway. A little dancing by the sea and Peavey will be eating out of my hand."

I talked to Catherine from a pay phone at the Wynn Dixie store. She was worried about Marcelline. I said, not Marcelline. She said yeah, she's having trouble about this guy. I said Marcelline is indiscriminate. I said the sexually indiscriminate have lost the ability to convey a sense of privilege. I said they're always having trouble with the guy. Don't lay that shit on me, Catherine shouted. I'm not shouting, I shouted and customers looked at me in the chest-high booth where I stared into the sound-proofing perforations and at the chained directory in false concentration. Trouble with the guy? Catherine said. Let me tell you trouble with the guy. Marcelline, it seems, had read some French novel and wanted to give herself in the form of a pagan rite, some form of utter consent. Sadly, she picked a vacationing agent from the firm of International Famous and he insisted on peeing in her face. Marcelline was in seclusion, in disgust with the human race.

"Has she had a chance to scrub up?" I asked.

"Hey, go fuck yourself."

The line was dead. I wasn't making the best of the conversations. I don't quite know why, except insofar as it was part of this trajectory of declining hope which had gone so far in depriving me of what I formerly considered worth working for. For instance, I will soon be broke. Already, on the occasion of massive overdrafts, where once an obsequious vice-president would appear at the door, I now got an ill-tempered trainee with a pencil behind his ear who menaced my dog.

Then I thought, I could make Marcelline feel better about all this, about this terrible agent doing this to her face, with his thing, that agent. And by so doing, apart from placating my own humanity, I could wend my way back into Catherine's affections, even to the extent of her withdrawing her remark about my fucking myself.

3

AT TRUMAN AND FRANCIS there is a florist's shop in a building made of the kind of cinderblock that is bulged to look like rocks. The window is always fogged from the cool interior and it is run like a dry cleaner's, with a counter and cash register jutting into its greenery like a dock in the Everglades.

"I want something nice," I said, watching across the street as a pallid rock-and-roll band loaded equipment behind a franchised fun bin called Big Daddy's Lounge. "For a friend. A whole plant." I could smell cold flowers.

"Is this a special occasion, I mean something for which we might have a price arrangement or any of them good things?" An eighty-year-old woman ought not to talk that way.

"A friend," I said, "who's had an accident."

"Oh dear, what?"

"Peed on."

"What?"

"She got peed on."

I settled for a plant with blue flowers in a terra-cotta turtle; not settled, really. I liked the plant and felt good marching through the cemetery toward Elizabeth Street toward Marcelline's, a Christian soldier. I spotted Peavey ward-heeling in front of the library and waved without eliciting one in return. I felt uplifted in some way, taking a little something to a friend who had gotten it as we all have, though seldom so directly. Then I remembered Marcelline wasn't precisely a friend; and in fact, I didn't know her very well. Maybe I don't know why I felt good, beyond that the obligation of being a screaming mis-fit was gone, the onus of dirty money was about to lift off, and the simple motifs of poverty and Chris-tian vengeance were starting to back-fill their ab-sence.

Vengeance? It's so intricate, maybe no one else would call it that. I don't question it any more; any-one's sources are as mysterious as spring water.

Marcelline's house is on the dead end of William Street, what was the dead end until the fire depart-ment opened it on through for access to the wooden tinderbox houses of this old quarter, on through past the empty stables in the overgrown palm-shrouded field; so that what was once still as countryside now carried the tin murmur of Truman Avenue.

Marcelline came to the door just as my finger touched it. She had painted bright red circles on her face and was wearing fifteen or twenty rings. I could hear the radio and a teakettle at once. She said, "Hi you!"

I told her, "Fine," then I said, "Marcelline, you look just, just—"

She said, "Go ahead."

I said, "It's not that, it's—"

And she said, "I know. *I'm indescribable.*"

I can't quite recall; I believe, though, she told me to come in. I did go. We bumped in the woody smell of the hallway, her bright circled cheeks in that light and the teakettle screaming now over a Spanish-language broadcast out of Miami, Havana, I don't know. Machine-gun music.

She cried, "Is that for me!" And ran the plant into the little sitting room. She had a coffee can with a soldered spigot and babied the vegetable while I tried to figure out what I was doing there. I believed that it had to do with Catherine. The room was dim and the windows drained everything; the lines in the wooden floor ran off into the glare and you could hardly decide what was what.

"We had a plant with blue flowers in Oklahoma once. My mother took it into the cellar with us during a tornado. I had a *Peter and the Wolf* record and my mother had a handbag. There was this big groan and the house was gone. The plant was okay but I forgot the record when we moved to Tampa. This was on a Wednesday."

"What was?"

"When we moved to Tampa. My mother worked for a pirate-type-atmosphere restaurant. Then she was a target for a knife thrower, and ran an addressograph. Jack-of-all-trades kind of deal I guess."

When she sat down finally, she said, "What brought this on?"

"Thought I'd you know come on over see how things were."

"Well, they're not too neat."

"I heard about your accident."

"That's just the end of it. The trip to New Orleans was also ratshit. I stayed out at the Cornstalks and it was full of musicians. So, I spent the whole time taking cabs into the Quarter, where you can't get nothin any more, not even a beignet you'd want to eat. You're better off down on Canal watching traffic. I tell you, bad luck and trouble is getting to be my middle name."

"Well, that and a dime will get you a cup of coffee in any town in America."

"I just want to fix up my place and kick back for about a year. I want them to be able to put the story of my life on a Wheaties box. I'm sick of junkies and dancers and triggermen."

"They're not going to put your unnatural conduct with Catherine on Wheaties."

"It's not unnatural. You ever read this Sappho?"

"Not Sappho again. You get the right Greek and you can really cover the waterfront."

"I go straight and you see what happens. All over everything. I nail the guy where it does the most good and he starts to whine. Save it for the john, I told him. I don't like it. So, then he tore up my place and split. I'd like to find out whose agent he is and tell his clients."

"You know what happens when agents die? They go to ten percent heaven."

"That helps."

"Can I do anything?" I asked, very much in earnest.

"You're not any more together than I am, as I hear it."

"I know," I said, "but I've made a start. Just ask me and I'll help you out."

"I don't need anything. It'd be nice if you could get that agent off the key. He's drinking at the Full Moon Saloon and that is my bar."

"Consider it done."

Marcelline stopped fidgeting around and re-arranging and stared at me a moment, absolutely otherworldly in her red cheeks. You'd want her on your arm at some kind of fiendish ball. I resolved to take her to my seaside gala, given that I could succeed in organizing it; that is, if Catherine predictably refused me. Marcelline was a vivid primitive and that was okay with me.

"Catherine is sure that she's a survivor. I'm just a flashy cunt. But I know a thing or two. I know what's what."

"Such as?"

"I don't know, the street. How to stay up all night by yourself, fry okra without it getting slimy, tell when plantains are ripe. I can test coke more accurate than a lab even if it's ether or acetone base and repair furniture without glue. But I'm not absolutely sure I'm a survivor. I might be gone in the next reel."

"Well, I'll get the slicker off the key and you'll

have the Full Moon back. That'll be a step in the right direction."

There are people anyone knows who are at times stranger to them than Hottentots. *Peter and the Wolf* in the storm cellar. And for me, these strangers are dangerously simple obsessions, not durable necessarily, but certainly it can get smokey. A topless dancer tells you about her paper route in Indiana. A shrimper shows you his collection of Fred Waring records. But without that, maybe you're all by yourself. I saw an old drunk fall in front of the laundromat at Elizabeth and Fleming. He cracked his head open and made a terrible pool of blood. Someone seemed to know he wouldn't die of it. But I looked down through spinning air filled with frangipani and rock and roll and saw how quickly you are alone, how that can be shown to you in an instant. I think for a long time that it was my business to drive this into relief, that this was what I did for my time, poured blood from my head so that strangers could form a circle. The immaculate dream of touching and holding was shed and I stood, an integer, not touched; for nothing but power. I couldn't even name my dog. But there was something I wanted besides that; something as simple as to ache in the literal heart and chest for all of us who had lost ourselves as parents lose children, to the horizon which is finally only overtaken in remorse and in death.

I talked to a woman who told me nothing larger than the house going off in the wind and the move to Tampa and thought, Let us not try to see beyond these walls where we are taken up into the terrible stream. And then my heart could swoon from the smell of a cold-cream jar left open, a calendar with two pages needing to be turned, a handsome lady looking to get by but holding some hard secrets beautifully lacking in universality.

I thought, I can handicap the track on this whole shit-heel civilization and truck paychecks till doomsday. It's like taking candy from a baby. But I want that cracked thumbnail, the graze of wildly disingenuous eyes upon my own, breasts suspended in the frame of arms, and level thighs drifting toward each other into the dark.

Because then I'm happy. I wanted Marcelline as absolutely as I knew I would do nothing about it. It starts with a gesture you remember from somewhere else: a girl chipping the map of Czechoslovakia into the polish of her fingernail. And in my hope of immaculacy, my Catholic childhood enshrouded within, I brained myself with the thought of her pulling the T-shirt over her head, the skirt unwound, each leg over an arm of the chair. And yes, me, at the business end of where it counted.

I last saw my brother Jim at a mental hospital where he had a small, decent room with a poster of me on the wall and which, don't ask me why, I couldn't bear to see there. It was the famous one of me climbing out of the elephant to sword-fight the pitching machine. He had hospital corners on his neatly made bed, a toothbrush in a glass, paperbacks, and a spiral notebook.

We walked around the grounds and he gazed with happy awe at me and told his ineffable, funny stories about the other patients, stories told with the sense of humor that is the mirror of pain, the perfect mirror, not the trick mirror of satirists. We had a long talk about our mother and father, about Roxy and our uncles. Then I flew to Stockholm to do a show. Jim was due out of the bin in three days. A week later, full of morphine, he smothered to death on a plastic-covered mattress. I came home and the last I saw of him he was lying next to a Lithuanian, who, after eating cat food for three years in a Miami hotel, jumped out of its window. I said Jim was Jim and they filled out his tag.

I thought, they'll fill out mine and Marcelline's and Catherine's too; which thought makes you tolerate every creep on earth. And I considered how Catherine had had enough. Well, hadn't we all. You are always up against those who ask, Why go into it? and the smart set who tell you, musically, That's how it is.

Wondering what I am doing here makes me behave as I have, which is a matter of record. Like Ulysses S. Grant, it was an instance of a village crank being called by his Republic; I found myself in the consciousness traffic, hawking a certain ugliness on a cash-and-carry basis. It took me a little while to get the bugs out; and after that, I was lethal.

See, in Key West, we were an old family that had lost its money . . . Marcelline was at the window. I want her to open herself for me without this fashionably veterinary innocence. This stuff is wicked and sinful and everyone knows it.

Marcelline, *please*.

I buried Jim. The rest of the family did needlepoint of ineffectuality to show how we'd gone broke. Jim was in an open casket, deferring to barbarism that mattered to his friends and our family. There were beaucoup whores and sorry-looking junkies, past masters at turning blue, who marched to the casket and then didn't know what to do with themselves, chins abashedly on chests, and fingers laced over their lower abdomens. As always, I positioned myself among the mourners, third from the left. I saw the body for days without so much as being reminded of Jim, a real effigy. Then when Catherine was with me and the funeral parlor was empty, I saw behind the cosmetics and cold smell of the flowers, the same smell when I'd bought the flowers for Marcelline; well, I saw. I felt something physical rack through and Catherine took hold of me. And I had this thought which was, I guess, a watershed: That's him all right and he's dead.

But once you get the idea finally that what dead means is the end and no one is coming back, once you know that as opposed to having heard about it and having coppered your bet with a few well-chosen coins of stupidity, then you don't care so much about your own any more. I don't anyway.

"I can't see why you brought me flowers."

"It was an impulse. I think I'm trying to get close to Catherine again. And she cares about you and for example worries about the wrigglers in your cistern as well as her own. But the flowers are just for you too."

"Are you jealous of us?"

"No."

"Because it's just this little thing, you know."

"Okay."

"I gather that at the end there you just went slap impossible on her."

"I did that. I believed myself though. I thought if I turned myself into enough of a goblin, everybody would come out and say what they had on their minds. Ha ha ha. What did I know."

"And gettin paid a lot with all kind of trash goin after you. Which you loved."

"I didn't hide that."

"And bringin it back to Catherine until there wasn't any pride left. New York chippies high-siding her."

"Yes, it was very bad. Is she gay now?"

"We're all just sick of you."

"You didn't know though how grand it was to go home to somebody who knew you for the asshole you were, that relief."

"Well," said Marcelline, "it got old."

"Sure."

"For instance you coming in with these flowers to do me up."

"That isn't true. I came because I felt badly about what that clown did and because I felt guilty that I thought it was funny. And I wanted to surround Catherine."

"She still loves you but I don't foresee her having a single thing to do with you. She put up with you right up to where you had become a real animal and a national disgrace."

"That was the height of my career."

"It was sick. You were a depraved pervert."

"Everybody calls me that."

"I wasn't going for originality."

"Did you ever turn tricks?" I asked her.

"For a little while."

I said, "How'd you like it? Turning tricks is how I saw *my* job."

"I dunno. This was out of a steak-and-brew joint in St. Augustine. It was real different, I guess."

"Strung out?"

"Yup, and sixteen. I was geezing speed. Later, crossroads and quackers. Up and down."

"Ever happy?"

"Quite often."

"Ever ask yourself what you are doing here?" I was waiting.

"All the time."

"How far do you get with the question?"

"Nowhere."

I started wandering around the place, halfheartedly looking for a spot to take a leak. I was off on a tangent. Marcelline held electrical fingernails to the light and I thought, Jim knew what ailed me but died and never said. And what ailed him? The horizon.

"The thing of it is," said Marcelline, "is that we want to talk and we want to fuck one another and if we fucked one another we'd talk better but we're not gonna fuck and I wonder how come."

I replied brilliantly, "We're being faithful to Catherine!" She smiled and then laughed like a valkyrie.

"Now and again," she said, "I see you looking at me and I can make out what you want and I feel bad about that."

"I'm not neglected."

"I mean, I'd do it."

"I would too," I said, "only we won't."

"I'm not even that sore from my trip, but I'm just not going to."

"It gets curiouser and curiouser."

"Did Catherine stay on the other day after I left?"

"Yeah," I said, "but it was kind of nothing, kind of flippant, kind of see-you-next-time."

"Everybody was confused after you nailed yourself up. I wasn't impressed with that particular lulu by the way."

I don't know what I cared to do at that moment. I really hadn't come for any but the described reasons. Which was not to say that Marcelline wasn't a leggy, otherworldly beauty, trailing her dubious dreams and pastel whoredom like a pretty kite.

When she picked up the phone, it seemed it could have been for anything. But she called Catherine. I felt immediately embarrassed, as though I had stressed the acquaintanceship with Marcelline into something I hadn't any right to. She told Catherine that I'd come over and been most, even more than, distinctly, a gentleman; but how would it be, now be honest, if she and I did get it on. It was perfectly all right with Catherine and I cannot pretend that that didn't hurt my feelings. I was worrying over things I hadn't cared about in years.

"Having it happen like this," I said, still staring

at the now inert and cradled black phone, "is flat strange."

"I've got a nice little cunt you're gonna be just crazy about."

"Fine, if I can. For years, I have to tell you, the only thing that excited me was to have someone fake an orgasm."

"Do you have a problem?"

"Just with suddenness."

"How about with guys?"

"I don't with guys."

"Scares you?"

"It's not there. Or I'd act it out. But I'm glad somebody likes it, so a possibility doesn't go to waste."

She was sitting in front of me, and put her hand up inside herself thoughtless as she talked. I considered the wonder of the things that befell me, convinced that my life was the best omelet you could make with a chain saw.

Marcelline tugged her top off and really started fooling with my mind. She loved herself and that just does it to me, pride of that kind.

She put some music on—*Tejas* by Z Z Top, I think, something hard—stood up, and slid out of the rest of her duds. I was transfixed, all my general views gone, everything withering to make room for the present, the furious rifle vision which riddles everything, that madhouse of what seems like a good idea at the time.

I had come with the flowers in addition to my usual maladies, been touched, and now found myself just as addled as thrilled. My mental focus left like water for her to swim in; and suddenly we were on the floor and she was slipping away and I'm thinking, I can settle this. And then I thought about Catherine and how it could be when it was with someone you loved. This was the girl from the storm cellar.

She said, "You've got premature ejaculator written all over you." I glanced into mid-air.

I felt completely there for it; but the feeling of the inside of her ran up spreading through me like swallowing hot soup upside down. I looked down, as I do, and thought, as I am afraid I do, that she couldn't get away. But she had some little movement that ought to be against the law. And I was grateful, wondering where my old vanity had gone, when it was always my benificence that I thought was on the line, not these glorious collisions. The earlier theater between Marcelline and me evaporated and it all grew dead serious; and probably, objectively, maybe even a trifle grotesque, as in knotty and wet and uncoordinated.

About then Catherine walked in.

She said, "I'm just so sorry but I can't help it and I don't know but I'm hurt." And began to cry. I rolled back. Marcelline stood up, that preening quality gone so that she looked a little gawky with defeated breasts and foolishly decorated cheeks. As for me, I felt elegant. I hadn't forced or even thought about the possibility of this disclosure except when hurt at her handing out permission. Now I was flattered and happy and wanted to take these lovely women to dinner and use my genius, which I have, to make them happy.

"Do you feel betrayed?" Marcelline asked Catherine.

"It's just that this spastic cocksucker was once my old man and I've got some reactions left."

I said, "I love you."

"Well, I can't begin to process that."

Marcelline said, "He's all right to fuck."

"Yeah," said Catherine, "I tried it and you shut up about it. There's something inside of him nobody can face." I wanted to know what that was, though I suspected that my enormous evasions had culminated in some ghastly suck hole. Still, I had faced a lot. The occupational hazard of making a spectacle of yourself, over the long haul, is that at some point you buy a ticket too.

Marcelline looked distressed. She said, "I feel like sewing it shut."

"I just had to go and spoil it," said Catherine.

"He's been real wholesome. You could take him anywhere."

"Ever see him with his teeth out?" Catherine asked.

"Huh-uh."

"Take your teeth out, champ."

I did.

Marcelline said, "Jesus Fucking Christ."

Catherine shouldn't have asked me to do that. I was tempted to get creepy. I feel not the same with my teeth out and I look frightful and as if I had nothing to lose.

Catherine headed for the john and Marcelline sat in front of me and touched my legs. Catherine shouted, "Get your hands off him. If necessary, I'll ball him."

"Don't say 'ball'!" said Marcelline.

"Please be friends," I said.

"We are, in spite of you."

"I didn't try to make trouble."

"Cath, we had your blessing," said Marcelline.

"I know, sweetie, but I wasn't here and my mind was acting up and now the animal knows I'm still carrying this torch."

"Why shouldn't I know?"

"Because depraved perverts misuse personal information."

"Would it help if I put my clothes on?" I asked.

"No, think of yourself as an Arab tent boy. Oh, you are a lovely man."

"He is."

"But finally you're not good. You don't like people, you like mobs. You're a lovely mob-loving rotter."

I ruefully watched Marcelline dress. "I'll tell you what," she said. "I've lost interest. Why don't you all let me be for now. The both of you, *ándale!* Call me from El Paso."

So then, Catherine and I were walking down the street again like old times and I was happy. Even the bus fumes smelled good. A filling station had become a Cuban sandwich shop overnight and I was vastly charmed by that. And it seemed bracing that Marcelline had thrown us both out, the little whore.

"Well, how did you like it?"

"Whussat?" I asked absently.

"The nooky."

"Oh, good, great, very nice indeed." I was running this on savoir faire. Catherine was irate and I was completely happy over it. "You seem displeased. It's a trifle."

"Is it?"

"Yes."

"Every Thursday this marine biologist and I meet and fuck around the clock. Are you happy for me?"

"I've been murdered."

Here was one of my vices, but I'm bored without them.

Catherine was strong and smart. I loved her and she was the only thing I couldn't have. I knew that what she claimed to see inside me was actually there. She is not a liar. I am both a liar and a forgetter. Moreover, I feel it in there, a streak of something that's never gotten any satisfaction.

I used to believe that if I really blew my gourd with ladies, such things would be worked out in little-theater form. Somebody called it the twitching of three abdominal nerves. Who knows.

I was carrying her down the street in my arms with my tongue in her ear. She made me put her down. I took out my teeth and gaped at pedestrians. It was all like before and I had a girlfriend.

Question: was Catherine a looker? I think handsome at least. Certainly no traffic stopper. Her upper lip was a little turned back and mildly insolent. But she had silvery eyes, drawn in the corners. She looked self-owned, cheerfully fierce, and ready to rock and roll. In our time together, she was often stern with me. She said I used those old drugs too much. But, given the objective conditions of our lives, how can we avoid taking the drugs? It's our only defense against information.

When I was down and out and ugly, Catherine could hold me when no one else could, and keep on holding me when there was absolutely no one, including me, prepared to claim it was worth it. She left me when two things came together like an eclipse: I was in good health and had behaved unforgivably. When I thought about her wanting to get out, I can only imagine that the combination must have seemed a long time coming.

As for her penchant for telling the bald truth, I'm not sure that it is a virtue. Cooking did not interest her very much; I loved sleeping with her not only for her fanciful approach but for her fucking back. Sadly, the more legendary I became, the more I neglected this and everything else. We ended quickly in the Sherry-Netherland Hotel, down the hall from Francis Ford Coppola's majestic quarters, quick because of her power. She left and I who had become, among other things, ruthless, and an absolute cretin, thought at first—I who had ignored her—"I will die of this." I couldn't have been more of a pig.

Instead, I slobbered, wept, crawled, and from time to time called room service for kiddie plates and gin. I masturbated endlessly and in some instances projected Catherine in humiliating variations on Leda and the Swan in which the featured players were a gruesome wattled turkey, an ostrich; never a swan, just the worst, most terrible birds.

Before she could leave town, I caught her in the Russian Tea Room eating salad behind dark glasses. She was on something and I could tell the waiters had been having a problem. I had never seen her like this. I thought she was ruined and that I had done it.

I took her back to the hotel, walking her through a corner of Central Park where a Puerto Rican folk-loric festival was taking place. She kept saying, "Aren't they damned good?" In the morning, she showered and split, apologizing crisply for the trouble, leaving an afterimage of her burnishing her face with a cloth and cold water, organizing her purse, adjusting her stockings out of my sight, and leaving her smell in three out of four rooms like an avenging angel.

I yelled down the corridor, risking annoyance to the ministers and personnel of Francis Ford Coppola, *"Are we finished?"*

"You bet your life," she said and covered her face. Back in the room, I pulled a chair up to the radiator, sat with my knees to the heat, and looked at the asylum city. I began to try to summarize what was happening to me; but I could only think: *This time the pus is everywhere.*

We were still walking, taking in the chronicles of street repair from cobble to tar along upper William.

"By letting everything fall apart," said Catherine, "featuring your career and livelihood, are you attempting to demonstrate that such truck is beneath you?"

"It's not that, Catherine."

"They are totally beneath you."

"I disagree. I quit because I felt unpleasant. Demonstrating awfulness breaks down important organs and valuable coupons."

"You're addressing the multitudes again."

"Yes, could be so. It's reflexive."

She smiled, very slightly triumphant, but not unkind.

"You women," I said.

"Oh, boy."

"Dragging me down. Pussy, job talk, intrigues. You're not like the fellows, you cunts."

"Women the only trouble you had?" she inquired.

"No, slapped up a bit by the po-lice. Threats from Counselor Peavey. Other than that, it's pretty nice. Plenty of ozone. Catherine?"

"What."

"Have I become pathetic?"

"A little, I have to say."

"The other day there, was that a mercy fuck? I want to know."

"Yeah, a little mercy. A little auld lang syne and just enough bum's rush to give it an edge."

This crack got me hot. You watch it, I thought.

"There wasn't any edge for me," I said. "It was like fucking a horse collar. Fall through, you'd tangle your ankles."

I thought I was ready but she brought one up

from the floor and moused me good under the eye. She had more slick and wicked sucker punches than Fritzie Zivic. We walked on while my face beat like a tomtom.

"Remember that morning we went to get married?" I asked.

"Yes."

"Did we?"

"I don't think so. I can check through my papers if you'd like. But I don't think so."

We had now cut a pointless zigzag to Whitehead and ducked into the Pigeon Patio and got a table facing the Coast Guard station. We ordered a couple of wine coolers.

"You working Marcelline for tips on me?" she asked.

"Nope." I bit a thick Cuban cracker and it sucked all the saliva out of my mouth. I pegged the rest of it to a bird who carried it to a sewer grate and dropped it through. That one's going back to Cuba. "But I was on the trail."

"I can't have it, and if you knew the state I've been in, you wouldn't press."

"How's your love life?" I, a Catholic, asked.

"The last one is living in the Dominican Republic with his wife. She is a jockey. Every horse's ass should have his own jockey. I was raised to think women did not become jockeys."

"Why are you here?" I asked.

She said, "Can't buy a thrill. How about you?"

"Will you go for pain?"

"Hell, yes."

"How about hatred of dead losses and hope of something better."

"I'll buy it. Any others?"

"Yes, ma'am. I'd like to point out my inability to stand having nothing that began long ago. Also we have sickness in the head and my failure to name my dog. We have no money, enemies at every turn, nuns haunting my house, evaporating lists of friends, the dark, family dead, and dead this and dead that and killing everything and killing time—"

"Shut up you."

"Yes," I said, "I will. I want a doctor."

"So I don't want to hear this."

"If I had the right tubes I could have a baby. Get me a doctor."

"Oh fuck you."

"I just want to start somewhere," I said.

"So do I," she said and by now tears were pouring down her face. I was, I guess, choking.

"But do it my way. Admit to yourself that you wasted so much of your life that not enough of it can be saved to matter. Then pull into yourself far enough that you can stand it and hang on until it's over."

"*Oh, shit,*" she said from her tormented face, and got up from the table. I didn't have it to watch her go.

4

A BEGINNING I could make, an act of friendship, was to remove this sight, this agent, from the key. First, back to my place to collect my dear, spotted, nameless dog, sobbing and scooping meat mess from a tin upon which a beagle laughed at the world. I drew myself up and felt stern enough to stop this endless crying. I put my arms around the dog and thought, grit down. That's what Catherine does and she knows better than you about all this. I put the empty dog-food can under the sink and headed off to find the agent, that shitsucker.

I could have dialed the five sixes and got a cab across the island but I needed the walk to level off and attempt some alleviation of the sense that I was closing in on absolute zero. I began by congratulating myself on staying out of Roxy's life for a little while; and permitting her to make her own kinds of trouble without my interference. I had indeed elicited signs of life from Catherine. I had cheered Marcelline, I think, and was off now to improve her lot. And I had stayed away from cocaine, which has lacerated me like Swedish steel for longer than I care to recall.

I went in through the front of the Pier House and stopped at the desk, where a boy with a trained voice saw to the registry of guests. I told him that all I knew was the first name of this agent, which was Mory, and that he was a member of the firm called International Famous. I mentioned none of his proclivities. In the trained voice, I hear, "That's not enough for me to go on."

"I think you're hearing the name Mory as being all I know of this person and I think that you'll find the room number and even remember what he looks like."

When you are tired in a certain way you can say things like that; a matter of what is the least you'll go through with; and above all, how you are to be avoided if you have a mean streak.

Mory was taking a call at the poolside phone, aggressive in smart trunks, and his eyes bearing forward at the image of the person he was speaking to. I waited for him to finish.

"Excuse me," I said, "but we have a mutual friend and I'd like a word with you."

"What kind of a friend," he said, wandering to his pool chair. I had to follow.

"One who owes you the minimum of a lawsuit. Have you got a minute?"

.

"That's a very silky opening," he said, "but I'm always being sued. It's a testimonial to my energy. Every benefactor has his off days and mine make people bring suit. I don't like this heat. When I'm with Double S on the boat, we move offshore when the heat gets this gummy. Then we keep the boat moving. We keep everything moving. You look irritable. This almost makes me forget the heat which is terrific but it's not nice heat. It's like dandruff." He was very compact and he smiled with a crazy aggressive arc that showed how he saw all he wished for happening already in his mind's eye. He got up. "A cold shower. I gotta get the lead out. You want to talk to me, you're gonna have to yell it through a plastic curtain."

I walked behind him as he arranged a towel over his reddened shoulders, really arranged it, making each hanging end of the towel the exact length of the other. And he walked that way, staring at the imagined adversary. I could watch these special cases for hours.

He had a suite looking out on the harbor. When we walked in, he pumped my hand and I gave him a false name. "I'm edgy," he said. "I got this director, a cunt face. And his insolence is about to bust my balls. He's Pied Piper to all these gifted kids who always think it's a repertory company. But his fee is batshit and he wants my action. The lift is otherwise perfect. He has a house critic who sucks him off on every motion picture he makes and he has a gift. He's an art whore and I only like the regular kind of whore." Mory was getting more interesting and in some ways more appealing than that which he was about to get from me warranted. He moved around the room amid the Vuitton luggage and luxury denim piles and I watched him clean from the center of my ugly streak while he talked away with marvelous accuracy. "Now our hero of the youth with his picture-book beach home and his actresses for the hotels is sticking me up for half my fee on a picture which *I* conceived and upon which we had an airtight conversation indicating he was gonna flat-rate the cocksucker for a nice remunerative ride on the back end! The insolence! —You don't even know what I'm talking about. If it wasn't you, I'd tell it to the lamp." He climbed into the shower. I went to the window and stood in the cold metallic air from the vents and looked at the anchored boats and the silver tanks and the casuarinas on the island across the way, ugly inside. When he was out of the shower, he wandered along the Habitat block walls plucking grooming tools off the dressers.

I said, "I'm here about a friend of mine. Her name is Marcelline and I don't like the way you treated her. I want you off the key."

"You want me off the key." He didn't turn around. "Marcelline. Well, you can't blame me for that."

"I'm afraid that I do and you're going."

"I'll tell you what, my pal, she bored me. It was a question of getting the cattle to Abilene."

When I hit him my ugliness and weight were all there. I caught him in the back of the head and his face collided with the block wall. When he slid down it, he turned, his face not at all what it had been; and I had to lean to let him have it again, and snapped him back good. "Three hours or the next plane," I said, "whichever comes soonest."

"Let me give you an errand," he said, "that'll clip your wings good. Tell Marcelline thanks for the invitation but I'm not gonna be able to make it over for dinner tonight. *You* go, chum. She was making me a nice piece of fish. You eat it. Yellowtail and black butter sauce from her sad little hands."

"It sounds like you got caught in traffic. What brought you to our island town?"

"Chester Hunnicutt Pomeroy," he said. "I'm the guy who could breathe life back into him."

"I know him," I said. "There's no hope. He's in knots and nobody has anything he wants any more. You're gonna have to sell it, but sell it in Los Angeles. You're all throwing in your lot kind of pari passu, except for the kids—and send something to the critic. Make the ride silky for everybody. It's good business."

"You're magic," said the agent. "You're me all over."

"What you would like to be," I said, "I can make come true."

"There's only one thing I'd like to be."

"Let's hear it."

He grinned bleakly and said, "Runyonesque."

5

AT 3 A.M. there are cats on the ledges, diffident animals of odd hours who know the enemy is at his weakest right around then. When you walk the street at that hour you think you share something and you reach out, try to make a deal, to touch. But the cats remember and they run.

Catherine didn't mind. She knew better. Nor did she offer to demonstrate the five things she remembered from ballet when she was ten. She didn't rant about cucumber sandwiches, other beings, the Montessori method, or the Schick center for the prevention of smoking. Fundamentally, she didn't try to pet the cats. She understood that they'd clear out. A lot of people I know would reach and then find that space on the ledge, rotten shitsuckers who had no right to pester cats at three in the morning.

"Let's buy some ammo," I said.

"Too late. What do you want with ammo?"

"I feel strangely Hessian," says I.

When we got to the corner of Duval and Caroline, some people sat on the wall and played various instruments. Catherine and I sang for them and we weren't too god damned bad.

Catherine limped around in time to the music. I removed my teeth. We commenced hopping up and down. I combed my hair with my bridgework. Ya-ya-ya-ya, say hello to the mayor of New York ya-ya-*yah!*

Well, we were having a nice time out there. Certain abuses of our expectations were at arm's length. No one clamored for encores. They stared at me and tried to put two and two together.

We lined up at the taco stand. "I hate lines," I said.

"Nothing you can do about them," said Catherine. "Not if you want a nice taco."

"I do. I want one."

"I want a messy one."

"They put us in mind," I said, "of our neighbors to the south."

"Don't be cavalier."

"After this let's go down to the fuel dock and decode the sky."

We carried our tacos to the Gulf filling station. Avoiding interference from ambient or stray light, I was able to identify the Big Dipper, for Catherine. "Contrary to popular opinion," I explained, "the Big Dipper did not die in a plane crash with Buddy Holly." I was straining for laughs.

Catherine said, "Thomas Jefferson picked out the site of Monticello at the age of ten."

"The Borgia Popes had a phone in every room," I replied.

"At the bottom of the sea, the fish have no eyes," she said.

"Did you get that from that low-rent marine biologist?"

"Everybody knows it."

"You got it from him, that seagoing wage ape."

"Watch the words, Chet, the words."

Cats fell from the tree in mortal combat. We stepped aside and they pinwheeled past. The pilings throbbed to hidden currents. I looked at the sad water and remembered when I wanted, because of the Saturday matinee, to run away as a cabin boy and find Charles Laughton's blubbery Old Salt Wisdom to guide my future to a sun endlessly falling into a shining sea, the old whale road where flying fish spangled the surface a square mile at a time and where, basically, seldom was heard a discouraging word. Instead . . . well, you know how it turned out. Substitute cyanide for sea; and curtains of remorse for all the flying fish in heaven.

I noticed that many people I saw were surrounded by invisible objects. Many of the visitors from New York had invisible typewriters right in front of their noses upon which they typed every word they spoke. Boozy hicks played an invisible accordion as they talked. Hip characters stirred an invisible cup of coffee with their noses as they spoke. Senior citizens walked down the street, dog-paddling in turbulent, invisible whirlpools.

When the sun came up, we were behind the A&B Lobster House. I was splashing water out of the bilge of my little sailboat with half a Clorox bottle. Catherine was hanging over the bow dangling a string in the water. She said the ripples made the reflection look like she was holding electricity.

"That time in the Russian Tea Room, what were you on?" I asked.

"I don't want to talk about that."

I uncleated the centerboard and dropped it. It knocked under the hull. I looked around at the well-built little sloop, proof that I was not an utter damned fool; as a matter of fact, the only one in a shipbuilding family who could still build a boat.

I stuck the tiller into the rudder and freed the lines that attached us to the decayed dock amid bright Cuban crawfish boats piled with traps and styrofoam markers. We began to drift away from the dock. Then suddenly I reached for the lines and tied us up again.

"I don't want to go sailing," I said.

"Why?"

"I feel like sinking it."

"We've been walking around all night. You're too tired."

"Breakfast," I said.

"My nerves are raw," she said. "We'll have to go someplace where the service is fast or I'll jump out of my skin."

Two dogs I knew, Smith and Progress, stared at

us from the breakwater. Shrimp boats were starting
to roll in from the night with their trawling booms
swaying to the same rhythm as they passed each
other in the channel going to different basins. A
panhandler appeared from behind the warehouse
and dismissed us. I was beginning to sense that the
night had written a check that daylight couldn't
cash.

We ate our grits and eggs faster than you could
say Jack Robinson. The radios were starting out of
the upper windows with the rising sun and shatter-
ing our nerves. Crazed bicyclists raced up Passover
Street with morning milk. Someone blessed himself
behind louvers. Catherine and I embraced wearily to
a Coast Guard weather report. I had the odd thought
that I couldn't fake a laugh for all the tea in China.

A Navy Phantom decelerated overhead in an
afterburner smudge and the entire shore of the island
seemed to close around my neck. In a moment, I had
trouble getting my breath. Catherine said, "What in
God's name is the matter?" My hands went to my
throat and I began to sink. "Straighten up," she said,
and swatted me on the rear. My eyes cleared and the
perimeter of Key West fell away once more. Nylon
Pinder materialized and said, "Want to try the
breathalizer?" There was weird light on the yellow
line.

"Get out of here," Catherine told him. "I mean
now."

The last time I went to Catherine's house, I was
welcomed. We got into bed and tangled up in each
other and slept in the sunshine in achy peace. I
dreamt of the Easter bunny. He gave me a sugar egg

you could look into and see God's own front yard. That seemed a long time ago. But I'm still walking around.

"Want to go to the library and deface Sandburg's life of Lincoln?" I inquired.

"No."

"It is characterized by Hoosier traits," I said.

"Sandburg's or Lincoln's?"

"A little of both."

"Let's visit Roxy and see how she is getting along."

"Do you want to, do you think?" In our condition, this seemed dangerous.

Right on Angela, where all the bottles are set in dripping cement, Catherine spotted a young man in a shiny suit. She spun. "Can't you leave us alone." He stopped, bobbing slightly on his web shoes, then ran off. I had the sense that they were coming in on us.

"He's got his nerve."

"I don't understand that at all," I said.

"There's a time for everything. I'm not a peeping Tom."

"I think you are."

Roxy greeted Catherine, then cut her eyes up at me and said hello. We walked out in back and sat beneath the divided fruit trees. I don't know whether Roxy could see us trembling or not.

She said, "I'm pleased you've come over. I'm getting a lot of infuriating phone calls about Peavey. I know Peavey wants that land. What does that matter to me? The Old Island Restoration Committee says it will become a Holiday Inn. So what? Have you ever had their clam plate? I find it very edible. Besides, whatever his motives, Peavey is attentive to me. Tonight we're going to *Deep Throat*. Day after day, he amuses me with his mindless money-grubbing and comic lack of ethics. Why should I worry about his getting my land?"

"Is he a Hoosier?" I asked.

"I don't think so."

"An out-of-towner?"

"I couldn't say. The trouble is, there are only about six on the plate, it's not enough."

"Six what?"

"Clams."

"On the Holiday Inn clam platter?" I asked.

"Don't make me repeat myself."

Catherine went over to have a word with the young man at the fence. When she came back, Roxy asked her who it was. Catherine explained that it was a private detective. Roxy said she thought we were already divorced.

"He's helping Chet keep track of his actions."

Roxy said, "It's a little late for that."

A jogger stopped to catch his breath and went on.

"There's only one thing to concern yourself with as applies to me," Roxy said deliberately. "After years of enthusiasm, I am almost devoid of interest. I'm sick of everything. The only response I can elicit from the family is greedy irritation. Finally, it's the only response I want."

Outside, Catherine said, "I'm so damned tired

and your aunt's personal philosophy is the tiredest thing I've ever heard."

"You can see how she got that way though. Besides, we asked for it."

"You're not like that and you've got more reason to be."

"Well, she keeps rolling. She keeps focused on the next thing. Collapsing into the present would kill her. I think she's hilarious."

"Do you get chills when you're exhausted?"

"Yes, and I drop things and my knees ache."

"Why don't you give up?"

"What?"

"Why don't you give up. If I were you I'd give up." Her cheeks were mottled from exhaustion. "You have nowhere to go but down."

"And you?"

"At the last minute, I'm going to drag myself tooth and nail to the bus station."

"Memories will assail you before you get to Key Largo."

"Your brain is decomposing," said Catherine. "I can smell it from here."

"I want to garner kudos by manufacturing an artificial paradise of household materials."

"Sit here."

"Thank you. But won't the bus stop for us?"

"This is no longer the stop."

"It is now. Catherine, if you are positioning me for discourse, quit it. We're tired."

"Your father said to me that he should have never left you with the nuns. He should have handled things himself. He said that he let too many others do the things he should have done himself. He said he injured you and he wants a chance to make up for it."

"I was just another snack to him and now he's gone."

"He's not gone. Chet, you have to go back and repair these holes. You're not getting anywhere."

"He got me below the waterline. It's a tribute to my durability that I've lasted this long. Jim didn't. And it's a family legend that my mother died terminally pissed off."

A city bus pulled up and stopped. The driver said it was no longer a stop. I thought that was thoughtful and said so. I told Catherine that I was not keen to pursue this conversation, and that the wolf was at the door.

"*Stop talking like that.*"

"I have my version of events."

"Which is what?"

"Tiny funerals."

"Is that to say that if people don't suit you, you simply decide that they've died?"

"No, Catherine—"

"What about me?"

"You're still with us."

"*How much longer have I got?*"

"You've still got some time left."

Catherine got up and stalked into the blinding daylight. It seems I'm always saying the wrong thing. But when the birds of morning induce terror, no one is at his best.

Sometimes I wonder about box office. What makes good box office, you think. What if a depraved pervert throttled the weather girl, is that good box office? I don't know.

I have experienced disagreeable side effects in all my endeavors. Sometimes I look at a situation and know they're going to get me and I say to myself, I think I'll just go ahead on out of here. I don't want disagreeable side effects. It's the additives. There has been a commotion among the impostors and they have introduced additives.

Jorge Cruz arrived late in the morning to discuss the orchestra. He was distressed at my choice of location. How was I to have an occasion at the Casa Marina, which had not been operating for a quarter century, when the grass grew to one's waist, how was one to dance under such conditions, to his orchestra. How was he to explain this to his orchestra. Explain that they will get paid, I said. But how would they recognize that this was an occasion to which they were to give of their utmost. I would speak to them beforehand, I suggested, to see if they were of a mind to give of their utmost. No, no, there was no need of this. In this sense, an orchestra was a herd of animals who understood only the one vaquero; he would speak to them. Jorge, I said, do we have a deal? And Jorge promised me an orchestra which would give of its utmost in the deepest neglect and tick-filled grass of the Casa Marina. I said, thank you, Jorge; it sounds very much as if we shall have an occasion.

Around twoish the CBS news team appeared. I took out my teeth and with some forethought conducted myself as a screaming misfit, a little on the laid-back side. I explained that I considered that I represented not so much the middle of the republic that produced mass murderers but the part of the mass murderer who explained that he didn't mean anything, that he just wanted to get out of town. I pointed out that poison dripping from a fang reflected the world around it as well as a virgin's tear. It was basically a walk-through. The commentator said he thought that I was "sick" and that my "corruption" was surpassed only by the "corruption" which had produced me. At this point, I fell completely silent, which is hell on commentators. I got a bit of goading and then boy did he have to talk fast.

Catherine turned up with her bathing suit, a towel, a lunch pail, and *Pale Horse, Pale Rider*.

"Could I sunbathe here? The Pier House is full of kids pissing in the pool. —Here."

She handed me a document in the Spanish language.

"What's this?"

"A marriage certificate. It's Panamanian."

"I don't get it."

"You asked me to check if we had gotten married."

"This is ours?"

"Yes."

"Panama?"

"I don't remember either." She walked into the water leaving her belongings behind, pulling her elbows into her sides at the chill. "I'm going to swim out," she said. "There's a sergeant-major fish always at the bottom of the piling. Saw you on TV this morning, champ. You were cuter than a speckled pup."

I walked inside to call Roxy. I was a married man. I walked back out and called to Catherine. "What year is that?" She couldn't hear me; so I looked myself: 1970. I had been married for years but I couldn't for the life of me remember Panama, though I knew it to be very warm and green, with a certain number of coconuts and a sleepy way of life. Panama. Many hats have been manufactured there. And there's that canal!

I walked in once again to call Roxy and got her. She sounded like a bad day at Black Rock, gargling into the phone incomprehensibly. The housekeeper took the phone from her.

"What's the matter with Roxy?" I asked.

"Her medication isn't suitin her so good."

"Is she okay?"

"Mister Peavey say he keep an eye on things."

"Where's Mister Peavey?"

"He livin in the front room by the radio. His secretary livin in the Flawda room."

"There's no bed in there, Mary."

"She say she plenty comftable on the terrazzo. And thass the room we can't get rid them palmetto bugs. Mister Peavey had his own phones installed and got a heap biness frins be's here all hour the night. So Roxy not up to scratch way she do most the time."

I hung up and turned around to Catherine dripping across the patio. "Flirt," she said. "Who're you flirting with?"

"Person named Mary."

"Spread it thin, do you."

"Spread it however I can."

"Do you."

"Yes."

"Got anything to read around here?"

"Not much."

"You flirting asshole."

"Oh, stop this."

"What's to read? Anything on Jenny Churchill?"

"Science."

"What?"

"Got some science books. Quasars, mound culture, stress in plastics, black holes in space."

"Have you got anything human around here, flirt face?"

"Dog books close enough?"

"I'm going to hit you in the mouth, you fucking flirt pervert."

"Oh come on, Catherine. Rinse your hair. It looks like linguini."

"I'm sick and broke."

"No more tears, we're off that now, off tears, so stop. What do you mean, you're sick?"

"I don't know, everything, gee, I—"

"Oh come on sweetie my God what is this?"

"I told that marine biologist I wouldn't see him

any more. He was in Coconut Grove on sopers and not acting right. He said you have to. I said no. He said yes. Then he began to destroy a chair over the phone to prove he was serious. I said no dice and he started smashing and a piece of chair went through his eye. The one he looks into the microscope with. Is it my fault?"

"Absolutely."

"*What?*"

"You produce these demonstrations as testimonials. It's a mainline cunt caper."

"I want some god damn solace from you, Chet."

"I'll give you solace. The marine biologist is blind in the eye he looks into the microscope with and it's your fault because you demand testimonials."

She shrieked, "You're making me crazy! Can't you help?"

"Buggery."

"*What?*"

"Buggery."

"Oh my God."

"I'll put tongs on your temples you screaming testimonial-seeking harridan."

Catherine hit me in the side of the head with a lamp and yelled, "Couldn't you have left me alone you sonofabitch. Couldn't you have left it clean like I did instead of running me down until I was nuts!"

I was crawling in the glass. The blow in the head had done something and I was seeing double and my hands were bleeding. Catherine sobbed, her face into the concrete wall, and I was dazed and my teeth were lying on the bloody tile floor. I ran my thumb over the bridge of gum where they fitted to see if there was any broken glass there before I put them back. I couldn't see how you could hire an orchestra and have this on the same day.

I went to Catherine and touched her and my hand made a bloody print on her back. She turned to me, her eyes nearly closed and only white showing in the openings, making her seem quite thoroughly insane.

Catherine needed to lie down so I put her in the mildewed bedroom and tucked her in. I hunted for something to read to her but could only find Fenimore Cooper's *The Prairie*; and not in an ideal edition. It was a Classic Comic. When I got to the end of it, having removed my teeth to recite all the Indian parts, I read the peroration: "*Abiram* was led away to receive the cruel justice of the desert law. The others made their way back to the settlements under the protection of *Hard Heart* and his *Gallant Band*. The *Aged Trapper* was content to remain and pass the few remaining years allotted him in the great reaches of the open prairie."

Catherine was asleep. I could see the ocean from the window and I let it blot into my vision. I felt all the emptiness I call home.

6

THIS YEAR the visitors from New York are a bit more homogenous than I had recalled. They wear their hair short and have clipped, British-military mustaches. They look orderly and reliable. Of an evening, they bump their bottoms frenetically to the music of sleepy or angry colored people; one song I hear all the way from Duval Street goes *"Don't do me no damn favor, I don't know karate but I know the razor!"* promising a bloodbath to the bottom bumpers on the patio, with timed James Brown grunts and *"Hep me now"* and *"Good God!"* coming out of the quadraphonics to five hundred screaming clones in dripping batik, coiffed like leftenants out of *Goodbye to All That.*

Thinking of moving again. Problems. Have to learn a new zip code. Still, I'm listless, too tired to work on my tan. And I'm wondering if I'm getting herpes simplex again. This morning I stared at my cock through a stamp collector's glass, looking for the little blisters on the pink distortion. I started to drift off as I stared through the glass. The little craters made me think I was on the moon. I reflected upon our country's space program. For some reason, scarcely anything seems to bespeak my era so much as herpes simplex. Oddly, it appears as—what?—a teensy blister. Then a sore, not much, goes away, a little irritant. It's infectious. When your girl gets it, from you, it is not at all the same thing. For instance, she screams when she pisses. She won't put out. She demands to know, "Where did you get this one?" The answer is: *From the age.*

I don't want to move any more; and maybe failure will bring some humanity to this situation. They no longer have my house on the tour; though Tennessee Williams's still is. The garden club brochure said the furniture was Cuban Victorian and Miz Somebody Or Other said *See it!* It idn't gonna be on the tooah next yeah! Cousin Donald Singer at the Greyhound freight office said Cuban Victorian was anything the termites wouldn't eat.

Also, I like being in a place where many of the people speak a language I don't understand. Then you begin to enrich your life by imagining what people are saying. Years of touring has given me this predilection. For instance, I perceived in the Russian tongue the history of the manufacture of galoshes. In the Spanish language I perceived the history of a lack of rain. I perceived in the French tongue the history of no underpants and an excess of utensils, both shaving and cooking. Who knows what's in American; farting, whistling Dixie, I don't know.

I went out for what seemed like a last-minute meal, a restaurant on the boulevard. Last minute before what I don't know. A heavy wind, screaming in palms that were stretched out over the highway. Inside I was alone except for two yachting couples dining together. Since they ruined my appetite, I will record their conversation:

"Can I have the buffet?" One of the women. She saw me and winked.

"Honey—" The husband caught the wink.

"Can I go to the buffet?" She studiously did not look at me.

"Honey—"

"G'outa my way. I'm gna buffay." She arises for me.

"Take it easy." He snatches her into her chair.

"I'm gonna have a roll and butter."

"Wait till they bring *the baron of beef for Christ's sake.*"

"Oh, you—"

"Okay, honey." The husband glared at me in challenge. He looked like a very stupid elk in Yellowstone National Park.

"I'm gona the bar, you."

"*Stay where you are.*"

"I'm gna the bar."

"Like hell you are."

"*You . . .*"

The waitress came. I tipped her but refused to order.

"I'm a woman."

"Right, honey," said the husband, rolling his eyes only very slightly.

"I'm a lady and you'll never get another one."

"Sure—" He bounces his fork tines very precisely against the table.

"And we're having a great time."

"This we know." He rolls his eyes for me. Now we are in cahoots. We agree his wife is a drunken slob.

"And I'm a wom—*auhbrappp*—woman."

"Exactly."

"So lay off."

"Okay." A sigh.

"And I love the sea . . ."

I went ahead and ordered a drink, big belt of Beam's Choice, and listened. The first thing I heard the woman say was "*Nnnnnrrughp!*"

"Oh boy."

Then a long silence while they waited for someone to bag their dinners.

"Gawd, I love us!"

"You better believe it!" One of the men.

"I honestly really love all of us."

"Right . . ."

"I'm a woman and I love the sea. Which is good."

"*Thin* . . . slices of beef . . . *English style*. In a bag. It doesn't seem right."

"The main thing about me *NNNGRUUGPH!*"

Everyone but the wife jumped away from the table, holding napkins at the ready. "Miss . . . oh . . . miss, uh I've made a mess. God I'm so sorry. Jese what a pig I am."

I left. Shitsuckers.

There is something to be said for lining up a few cheap thrills ahead of time. As I grow older the cheapness is easier to come by; but the thrill is always the same twitching of half-shot nerves. My father is dead and he wasn't any help to me anyway; but he was the only one I had and so at night I walk around and think I'm talking to him because he came from some place and was born in a certain year and he was my old man and he died in a certain year, as always, while there were still things to be said. And really, all I wanted to say was, So long, Pappy, I know it's a lot of shit too. And whatever I might say about you as a father, you're the only one I got. Still, you didn't treat me like you should have.

But what I line up ahead of time is an imaginary stroll with him through some unsuspecting neighborhood, the old man's face suspiciously Indian, blunted with vodka, turning to every detail in the street, nothing missed, no gaiety lost for knowing that it all ended badly.

Sometimes the stroll is down in the Casa Marina with the plywood gothic facades and the terrible sigh of air conditioning in the jasmine. Yet at the end of a street, the ocean will roll toward you hauling its thousand miles with a phosphorescent pull. I note an

odd detail here and there, but my old man would be
the one to spot the banker's wife staring in an upstairs mirror, waiting for the scream to start in the
shag carpet. Nevertheless, it was all acceptable to
him; he would shrug. Drunk enough, he would turn
his head between his upraised shoulders and look for
the next instance of the disease, something crooked,
the smell of a child's run-over puppy hidden in the
garbage, beginning to turn in the heat. Or simply the
suddenly unkempt lawn of a young couple learning
to watch the dream vanish. As my life quiets down,
menaces begin to appear, and whether I'm inventing
them or they are real doesn't matter to me.

I stand for those who have made themselves up.

I am directly related to Jesse James. That is
true. We were out of Excelsior Springs, Missouri,
and hid him in our barn more than once. I have
played in that barn, and in fact, it is within the
gloomy space beyond the hay mow where Jesse
James is supposed to have hung upside down, with
his percussion Colts in his trousers. Cole Younger
didn't have his black impracticality, and while Jesse
disappeared mysteriously with his beard in the nine-
teenth century, Cole Younger shaved every day and
timed quarter horses on the brush tracks of Missouri
when nobody knew what a quarter horse was.
Everybody in my family lived on the edges of the
Civil War, Key West, and the bloody borders; we
couldn't live on the main line. But we fought shitsuckers whenever we found them. My maternal connection, on the Jesse James side, owned an interest in
a foundation horse still talked about, White Light-

ning, stolen out of Reconstruction Tennessee and taken to Missouri. If any of this is not true, I will say so. Two men came out of Tennessee to reclaim White Lightning and were not heard from again. There was a cloud on the title forever. All of this horse's progeny were running fools, sorrels and chestnuts. My grand-uncle said that when they would come into the barn out of the rain to shake themselves dry, it sounded like thunder. And that was how you knew they could run. He said that if Jesse James had had colts out of White Lightning instead of just grade horses and plugs, he would have been governor of the state of Missouri. I personally think he was someone who could not live on the main line any more than me or my fairie uncle. And I'd like for nobody to find that out the hard way. White Lightning's get came to one hundred thirty-six live foals; and the prettiest one, a chestnut with a blaze face, kicked him to death in a Missouri corral.

They could all run.

We want a little light to live by. A start somewhere. Little steps for little feet. Or even something commanding, scriptural or mighty. I myself am discouraged as to finding a hot lead on the Altogether. Like every other child of the century deluded enough to keep his head out of the noose, I expect God's Mercy in the end. Nevertheless, I frequently feel that anybody's refusal to commit suicide is a little fey. Walking about as though nothing were wrong is just too studied for the alert.

There was a writer on Elizabeth Street who had had some success and broke down or burned out. We drank together once in a while in a bar whose owner had nothing more to say for himself than that he had thrown Margaret Truman out for disorderly conduct. He enjoyed needling the writer on crowded nights when the writer liked to stand up to watch the band playing.

"Down in front!" The owner.

"I can't see sitting." The writer.

"I said, Down in front!"

"Get fucked!" The writer.

"Line up!" The owner.

The writer fired a beer bottle at him and the owner put the bouncers on him and unloaded him on the sidewalk. The writer and I walked toward Captain Tony's in the meringue night amid the social terrors of our epoch. The writer said, "I'm not going through with it, this work of mine. No one believes in it, least of all me. You're a mess too." I told him it was the age.

"Well," he said, "the age is breaking my balls. I'm going home."

"Why are you telling me this?" I said.

"I had a friend, he took the scissors to his face. My sister's a dead zombie in her twenties because of your fucking age."

"If you picked me to stand up for the Republic, you got the wrong Joe." I thought this was hideous, railed at as though *I* wanted any of this frightful shit-heel madhouse.

"I been thinking about you," says the writer. "You and your trashy friends laying waste to our mythology. You're gonna choke on it, you smut-mongers."

"Keep it up, I'll tear out your windpipe."

"Let me buy you a drink."

The Whistle Bar: the bartender is talking into mid-air. He's an old friend and won't let people bother me. Also, he keeps pushers off me on a specific basis. He won't let them give me coke; whereas a Percodan or Eskatrol guy can get through. The next week, the diet changes. "I'm glad the college girls have gone back," raves the bartender, "I don't want any more pussy. I don't want it, I don't like it. I'm fuck-foundered. I'm to where if I was with Miss World, I'd lose my hard-on over a barking dog. I'd rather dynamite shellcrackers on the Caloosahatchee."

The hotel across from the post office burned down that night and we watched the inferno from the balcony drinking straight Lemon Hart on ice. I filled my mouth with one-fifty-one and hung out over the tourists and blew a flame into the night, a flame from my mouth to encourage the burning hotel to leap the street.

The writer said, "I'm a goner, see. So, I'm willing to help a new guy."

"I'm not a new guy," I said. "I'm Swiss cheese."

"Shut up you mouth. You might write someday. Your memoirs. The overnight sensation. You may turn to immortality to keep from looking down the street. The immortality of an artist, you should know, consists in the lag between his death and the time his collected works are flushed down the loo. I got the title for your memoirs, chum, and I been carrying it like a hot potato till I could run into you. I want you to call it *Eleven Ways to Nigger-Rig Your Life*."

He had a piña colada in his bony surgical hands and he held it up like a chalice attempting to watch the burning hotel through the milky glass. I went home and wrote a letter to my brother Jim on the Olivetti. Then it seemed that I couldn't read what I had written. And hours passed. I don't know, you just drift away. Then you can't wake up. It's the middle of the night, no-man's-land. They're all laughing at your handwriting. It seems like a small thing but you suspect that it will kill you. One thing leads to another; daytime arrives on an evil wind. You can't get your hand off the doorknob, your teeth out of the girl's teeth. Increasingly, you can't remember anything and you are suspicious that perhaps you shouldn't. In the end, your only shot is to tell everyone, to blow the whistle on the nightmare. It will work for a while; no one knows how long. The worse the dream, the more demonstrative you must become.

I took to the stage.

7

I CAME HOME Wednesday night loaded, having had enough of the writer. An isometric bull with the jaws of a wolf was guarding the door to the patio. So I knew I needed coffee. It was raining.

The instant coffee dropped in veils through a fathom of hot water and then a cockroach fell off a framed recipe into it and drowned. I flipped him out with a butter knife and bethought myself of change and a new life.

O Catherine, don't leave your dead meteor! I'll be better for you and the weeping will end. I'll be better for you and the weeping will end.

Yet when I awakened, something still hung over me. I went over to Francis Street for bollos and coffee and was taken aside, right on the sidewalk, by a man who wanted to know if I had any angles on local attics. He was a collector of everything but especially of barbed wire and Orange Crush bottles. He had the world's largest collection of early New Mexico burglar alarms and that wasn't even an area of specialization for him. "No attics," I said simply.

He said, "Take it easy, pal. I'm not gonna bite you."

I ate the bollos and drank the coffee. Back out on the street, I noticed something: my shadow was pointing in the wrong direction. I was walking toward the sun and my shadow was straight out in front of me.

Then the police pulled the big cruiser up alongside of me and kept it at walking speed until I nipped up Lopez Lane and bought an aloe plant for a dime.

When I got to Roxy's, all was not well with her. She was now engaged to marry Peavey and she was rolling around the floor, fully dressed, crushing a fine old straw hat with each revolution. I ordered her to her feet. She got into a kind of crouch and ran across the room into an armoire. That was the end of the hat. Then the phone book walked to the sofa like an octopus before it sloughed to a stop.

"What's the matter with you?" I asked. She got up and began to march. Her diphthongs seemed to last forever.

"*I'm never going to enjoy life,*" she said. "*I hate everything.*"

I got out of there.

They are raising the contents of a wrecked galleon below Key West, *Nuestra Señora de Atocha*. There is distress; for, in addition to the numerous pieces of eight, they are finding coke spoons. There has been an attempt to describe these as spoons for ear wax. They won't go in an ear. The divers knew what they were. They find jeweled rosaries and crosses; they find swords. The divers pay off bar tabs with pieces of eight. Where did all that coke go? And how much did this New World brain-raker have to do with the Golden Age of Spain?

They hauled two cannons up on the beach at the foot of Greene Street. Catherine and I went to look at them. The bronze was sea green and cast dolphins curved at the trunnions. The tops of the cannons were beveled flat and polished by sea turtles.

Catherine said, "Will they still shoot?"

"Where'd you come from?"

"I saw you standing here. I said to myself, 'What's he doing with those cannons.' And I'd been thinking about you."

"Let's go someplace and get drunk."

"It's nine o'clock in the morning."

"There's more than one way to skin a cat," I said. I wanted minestrone and Frankie Laine records, something other than this heat, the steady clangor from Mike Brito's shipyard, and the thought of Roxy marrying Peavey. I had no sudden ideas for making Catherine fall in love with me again; on the other hand, she wasn't leaving the key; and, given that she was out of work, I gathered I might, I said *might*, be part, I said *part*, of the reason she was staying.

I wandered into the street a little and Catherine

motioned me to the curb. I suggested going to the
bank and making a cash withdrawal and investing it
in party drugs. She was very much opposed to this
idea in all respects and, in fact, challenged the notion
that I had any bank account at all. I thought to nip
this one in the bud. She suggested that my short-
term memory loss was getting to be a problem to me
more than anyone else.

We went into my bank, a mozarabique mockery
at the foot of Duval Street. Most of the staff was
drinking coffee and arguing. One teller's window was
open and a line of more than twenty people wound
around the inside of the bank to this teller. Catherine
and I got in line and were there for a very long time.
A Cuban immigrant, a woman in her fifties, carrying
a plastic mesh bag with a can of Bustelo coffee in it,
arrived at the window and said something to the
teller in a soft voice. He looked out into the inde-
terminate space beyond her shoulder and said, "I
can't understand you." He was resting the point of
his pencil on the counter. He turned it carefully and
rested the eraser while she repeated herself.

"I don't speak Spyanish," he said. She said in
broken English that it was English. He said, "I don't
speak *your* English." The coffee drinkers glanced
over. "I can't understand *that*," he said to them. Then
he called down the line, "Any motel owners?" Two
signaled. They came forward and he collected the
take.

A heavy man in a plumber's shirt said, "What's
going on?"

The teller said, *"Banking."*

A short while later, I was at the cage.

"You don't have an account," he said. "We've been through this before."

Catherine said, "We're together. I'd like a current balance on my checking account."

The teller said, "Well, which one of you is it?"

"You've just explained that he has no account," said Catherine. "You answered that question. Here is my number. Get the account balance now and don't be a tired old bag for another minute."

"Oh, Miss California, are we?"

"No, you are."

"How would you like this in your face?" He picked up a calculator tentatively and Catherine started screaming that she was being attacked. The manager came to the door of his office and curtly summoned the teller.

Catherine checked her account with the next teller and withdrew some money. We went back out in the street. She was already thinking of other things. "I'd like you to meet your birthday present," she said and led me back to the La Concha Hotel. We went to the fifth floor and knocked on an unnumbered door.

"Come in."

"We can't."

"Why?"

"It's locked."

"That's why you can't come in!"

"Where are these people coming from?" I asked.

The door opened and a young man in a kind of shiny suit you scarcely see any more stood there and said, "Oh." And then said, "Come in." He reached out, his arm angled up and his hand angled down, and said, "How do you do. Don Hathaway." I shook hands. I would describe the contents of Don's room but none of it's of any interest. I know many people who would describe it anyway.

Don said, "I've been following your career for years and now I'm following you."

"What's this mean, Catherine."

"Don is a private detective," said Catherine. "I've hired him to follow you."

"To what end?"

"He is going to report to you every day everything you did the day before. As time goes by, he will report every two days and so on until you can remember on your own. Happy birthday."

"Your birthday was on Wednesday," said Don.

"How old am I?"

"I don't know . . ."

"Well, find out."

Because I hadn't spoken to the interviewer, they wild-tracked a lot of stuff from my old performances and played it over my frozen countenance, all with a mind to making me seem in bigger trouble than I really am. This had the effect of bringing idlers to the front of my house in hopes of seeing what was being peddled as the most sleazed-out man in America.

There was a kind of concrete fountain in front of the place with an iron egret rusting on a length of welding rod. I hung a sign on it that said:

DEPRAVED PERVERT WISHING WELL

and the money began to come in. It was clear that before the kids got on to the coins, I'd have enough to put on my party at the Casa Marina. Late at night, while I slept, I could hear the change plopping in the fountain and I felt happy. Still, I suspected that the law of averages would soon bring a justice-hungry citizen, some shitsucker, creeping into my place to avenge decency. Here though, I was confident my silent-running dog would have such a one by the leg. So I slept.

The next day, Don stopped by to tell me about my wishing well. He also told me that I was cavorting in the sand at Rest Beach at three in the morning. I told him he'd made this up. He said, "You cut your foot on a Doctor Pepper bottle. You'd better put something on it." I'd been limping all day. Don left. I got some mercurochrome.

Catherine and I lay in the sand. I was on my back feeling the sun form its evanescent oval on my belly, the hot retinal images that come through the lids. The sea was breathing at our feet and I considered how trying it can be to be crazy, with a Band-Aid on your arch, if you accept that you are that, crazy, which I had not, any more than I had dismissed it. I rolled over and rested my hand on Catherine.

"Cut."

"What?"

"Cut it out."

"Okay. What's wrong with that?"

"It's not wrong."

"Then what's this?"

"*I just don't want any.*"

"God why are you shouting? It was recently my birthday."

"I want some sun. And I'm thinking."

"About what?"

"About simply making a living. The cans are nearly empty. It's a photo finish every month, getting everything paid. And I have to admit, this private detective is just about all I can handle."

"Catherine, I didn't ask you to hire this private detective".

"He's the only legitimate expense I have. Don't start diminishing *that.*"

"*He's useless.*" I was shouting.

"I don't believe that."

"*He's absolutely useless.*"

"I bet he's already told you something you didn't know."

That kiboshed my replies good.

Catherine said, "Oh, please, I'm sorry. Why do I attack you? You haven't got a chance."

And then she slept dreamlessly while I watched her. I got up quietly and slipped into the house to dress. I walked down to Juan Maeg's store and bought a handful of tin rings with plastic jewels; and I bought a few dozen washable tattoos. I went back to the house, fished almost three dollars out of the wishing well under the disapproving gaze of fat Mrs. Dean next door, and walked around to the beach. Catherine was sound asleep. I haven't got a chance? I slipped the rings over each finger, licking them so they'd slide on without waking her. Then I got a dish of water and began tattooing her: Donald Duck, Spider Man, anchors, hearts, Dodge, Chevrolet, a nice Virgin of Guadalupe, the Fonz, an American eagle, the Silver Streak, Bruce Lee. I covered her and went inside.

When she came in a while later, I was conscious of what a spectacle she was; the tattoos were startling. I smiled a question and she said, "Let's eat." Then she started toward the door. The tide was turning.

"Don't you want to scrub up?"

"No, I'm fine."

She insisted on eating at the Pier House, which is a nice place, full at lunch, a professional clientele. We asked for a table, me in my huaraches and housepainter's baggy pants, Catherine in a bathing suit, twelve paste rings, and twenty-five loud tattoos. It was the last month of hurricane season.

Catherine wanted to discuss local Cuban politics. She didn't know anything about them and I couldn't get past how peculiar she looked. I asked her, "How can you do this to me?" The whole god damned restaurant was gaping. I felt like a fool.

We went back to my place and Don the detective was waiting for me. I found this distressing, since I'd already picked some songs to play for her on the mandolin. But then, it seemed she was waiting for a reason to slip off; and suddenly she was gone. Don got out his notes. I said, "I don't want to know."

"Don't waste her money. She works hard for it."

"No she doesn't. It's all in a can. What does she pay you?"

"Classified."

"You're not supposed to be here now."

"I won't be regular. That would only start your memory loping. I'll just pop up."

"I hate popping up. That's against everything I've ever fought for. Don't you fucking pop up on *me*."

Then he recited each thing I had done from bandaging my foot to tattooing Catherine. There were no surprises; but I didn't like the feeling I was getting. I didn't like it at all. I looked at Don. Today he was wearing mesh shoes and a banlon sport shirt. I could not fail to notice that he had moved his part from one side of his head to the other since the morning.

"I'm going to give you a little extra time," he said, "let you get in a little trouble with your memory. —See ya."

As he darted off, I sensed the air pouring into the tops of his shoes, his purely professional curiosity, the shifting part of his hair, and the utter menace of being up against someone who had a real memory he'd use on you.

It wasn't long before I began having a problem retrieving funds from the depraved pervert wishing well. As you know, I have been beset by impostors. Years ago numerous elephants lost their lives in Western Europe at the hands of people who had no idea what a batting practice machine was. An enterprising Frenchman emerged in Brazilian soccer clothes; but that wasn't the point. That odd young fellow, Chris Burden, who shoots himself, was closer to me and my elephant than these deluded Europeans. The main thing is that impostors have been my cross. The worst of them was at the well today.

I emerged from my home by the sea in shorts and drugstore flipflops. I was not anxious to run into anyone, as I had been making notes to myself that morning on my stomach with a ballpoint while I drank my coffee and greeted the new day. I hadn't had a chance for a shower; and I knew that from a stranger's point of view, I did look a bit like something from the *National Geographic*. At any rate, there was a stranger at the well. In human history, one of the most terrifying appearances is that of the stranger at the well. The truth is, if I had still been in the same business of my recent years, I would have included this in my repertoire. He peered at the upside-down map of the Lesser Antilles on my stomach, the word "Antigua" scrawled across my belly button. I really shouldn't have come out.

He was dressed in clean white ducks stylishly unpressed. A chambray shirt and a handsome old blazer. He wore deck shoes on brown sockless ankles. He was a well-groomed man in his fifties and he carried a small, heavy satchel that said "Racquetball" on its side. When I appeared, he reached inside and began throwing handfuls of silver dollars into the well.

"Now will you talk to me?" he said. "I am your father."

"This is a cruel ploy to take with an orphan," I told him. I wondered if he would ever find his son. He kept showering the silver dollars into the well, as if to say I would not talk to him otherwise. The pathos of this empty gesture is absolutely all that kept me there.

"You touch me with your desperation," I said. "And I advise you to roll up your pants and get your money back. You've got the wrong Joe." With this he angrily emptied the whole satchel into the water. I would never touch that haunted money.

"Now listen you sonofabitch. I haven't got all day. I'm going to find out if you're compos mentis before I go back to Ohio or know the reason why. I'm trying to have a well-earned rest on my yacht, which I have maintained at the dock for five years unused in anticipation of this holiday, and I'm pissing the entire deal away running down my birdbrain, notorious son who refuses to admit I exist."

It was quiet for a long time.

"Why?" I asked.

"Because it's all I want!" he said, and his voice caught. He turned away. He hurled the racquetball bag into the well and walked off to a waiting car.

So, you see?

8

    I DECIDED that if I was to break out of my present pattern of impoverishment, sorrows, and anger, and stop waiting for everything with Catherine to repair itself, then I would have to fly in the face of my instincts and perhaps discipline myself and do things I didn't want to do and make friends with Peavey even though he was robbing my stepmother of what was rightfully hers and ensconcing himself in her Florida room with his associates and his bimbo secretary. This was not going to be easy. This was going to be a bitch. But if I succeeded, I might begin to make sense to other people too.

    I got there rather early in the morning. Mary, the housekeeper, was sitting on the front stoop, drunk. I said good morning and she attempted a reply but could only make a bubble, though it was a good-sized one. I stepped past her and went into the house. I saw Peavey immediately. He looked up at me without acknowledgment, crossed to the Florida room, and closed the door behind him. He was dressed rather simply: a grimy pair of Fruit of the Loom underdrawers. When he opened the door, I caught a glimpse of his secretary rolled up in a sleeping bag and idly returning the empties to a six-pack carton.

Roxy was in the living room, legs crossed at her writing desk, looking smart in an off-pink Chanel suit. This set piece of normalcy was not going to take me in.

"Sit down, Chet, I'll be with you in a moment."

"Take your time."

"Bills, obligations, God."

"What's Counselor Peavey doing running around in his underwear?"

"Just got up. What's seven times nine?"

"Sixty-three. Was that his secretary in the sleeping bag?"

"Sometimes she's a secretary. She's kind of a late riser. Works late. If that little gal gets wind of the Equal Rights Amendment, Peavey'll have his hands full. —I thought so! The aqueduct commission has robbed me to the tune of two dollars and nineteen cents. Did you see Ruiz when you came in?"

"No."

"Well, he's selling my grapefruits. I'm going to skin that chiseler."

We could hear Peavey making not-quite-human noises through the door to the Florida room.

"What's he charging?" Roxy asked.

"Who?"

"Ruiz. For the grapefruits."

"God, Roxy, I've never seen him selling your grapefruits."

Mary walked through the room with a thin row of bubbles on her lips.

"What's the matter with her?" I asked.

"Get that fly," shouted Roxy.

"Roxy, what fly?"

"What fly? The fly walking through my addition practically into your face."

"I want to give you away."

"I think your father should do that."

"But I'm having a party at the Casa Marina," I said.

"Who's the orchestra?"

"Jorge Cruz."

"That's very nice. Jorge is very good indeed. Plays some attractive sambas—" Roxy got to her feet and began to samba. I could see her starting to get peculiar and I returned her to her chair.

"Don't start shoving *me* around," she snarled. "Not with *my* obligations you don't."

"I just wanted you to sit and talk to me for a moment."

"I've got a thieving gardener, a stack of bills like *that*, and a drunken attorney with an outside line consorting in my Florida room with some women's libber in a sleeping bag."

"Well, why are you marrying him!"

Peavey peeked out of the door.

"Who asked for your two cents?" he demanded.

"I just I . . ."

"*Nixon.*"

He withdrew.

       The usual pattern of mayhem in the morning paper was altered in the edition of *The Key West Citizen* I bought to forget the situation at Roxy's (where I had got no reply to my offer to give away my stepmother, in matrimony). A young couple living on Big Coppitt, having fun with morphine and Quaaludes, beat up their three-year-old son and threw him through the window; the little boy took seventeen hours to die. Page 2: "Hints for Shell Collectors."

       I walked to my place with tinned dog food, stepped into the patio, and said, "Deirdre" to my dog. I had named her, after seven years. I held out my arms and she leapt about, running on her hind legs. "Deirdre," I said, "Deirdre, Deirdre, Deirdre." And for a moment, page one's hint that the human race was in line for a fiery death, vanished.

       I looked out at the ocean, past the ruined pier where nothing was visible except Don smoking in the shadows. I called out, "Aren't you hot in that suit?" and opened a can of dog food. Weird guy, Don; he smokes Virginia Slims and carries his car and office keys hanging on a split ring from the belt loop of his gleaming suit. I have to study him as a means of keeping him at arm's length. A less patient man than me would pull all his teeth or something. When I looked out again, Don was gone, but his cigarette smoke was still in the air, quite visible against the quiet blue sea.

Beyond the wall, I could hear sunbathers talking and I eavesdropped on their senseless conversations. Deirdre stood beside me.

"Scarred for life . . ."

"Not excited . . ."

". . . nothing personal between us."

"Girl is getting me down. (I spoke to her of) . . . Rasputin, the Kalahari, the telegraphy of souls and ocean. All she wants to do is sixty-nine."

Then I went straight back to Roxy's, blood in my eye. I went to the outside window on the west side of the house, stood among the raped grapefruit trees, adjusting the garden hose. Peavey was dictating a memo to the bimbo and I let that shitsucker have it, squirting everything and shorting out the typewriter. Peavey said I wouldn't be able to say I didn't ask for it. His hair spread in vertical lines behind his glasses. There were puddles.

The morning mail made a terrific difference. Paramount had released *Chronicles of a Depraved Pervert*, which was good for a deferment of just about a half a million dollars. I wrote out a deposit, knowing I'd cover the check before it went through. Oh, boy. I went back to the same teller, endorsed and presented the check. "Call me when this clears."

"I shall."

"Break your balls?"

"It's only money."

When I got to the house again, the phone was ringing. I answered it and had a long, tormenting conversation with someone close to me, which confused me very much as it was someone I had long believed to be dead. My own unstoried dead are an important phase of my current balance and having them pop up like this produces unusual stress and an urge for mayhem. The living are skeletons in livery anyway. I'm not going for this. My first impulse was to wonder if they ever found Jesse James's body.

I bought a Land-Rover, and an attractive home for Catherine. She refused to look at the house on her own. I didn't feel I had the time; I had bought the place by phone and didn't want to be disappointed. She was tending to Marcelline again; Marcelline's fiancé—I didn't know she'd had one—was arrested in New Orleans for grave robbery. I thought this was a ghastly crime but Marcelline assured Catherine that many young musicians in that city survive by robbing the Creole cemeteries.

"I thought she hated the Cornstalks Hotel because it was full of musicians."

"One was right for her."

"One was right for her? What does he play?"

"What?"

"What instrument?"

"Moog."

This left me with an undeservedly bad impression of Catherine; and I called again and asked her if she would go up the keys with me in my new Land-Rover. We could go to No Name and see all the way to Little Knock Em Down. This touched her craving for actuality and she said, "Yes, oh yes."

I made crab-salad sandwiches and iced two quarts of piña coladas. I got a blanket and some bug repellent. I loaded everything into the Land-Rover and glanced across the street. For just an instant I thought I spotted Jesse James on the broken sidewalk.

I had some trouble with the Land-Rover in the beginning. While not a Road Ace, I am a good driver with illegal left-hand turns as my only moving violations. But the Land-Rover had a number of shift levers, high range, low range, transfer case; and when I looked in the manual, I found only the instructions for attaching sheep shears to the power takeoff. None of the gears were synchronized, and by the time I got to Catherine's, I had crashed the gearbox good. I slurped insistently on the piña coladas and peered about behind the divided windshield, idling with the controls.

Catherine climbed up and in, Marcelline waving from a curtain. All along the street, people had piled their dead palm leaves for pickup and the Spanish limes were dropping steadily on the tin roofs. We were on a gloomy side street with traffic flickering at either end and the sky high and oceanic.

I said, "It takes a rhino to turn one of these over."

"What is this?"

"A Buick."

"They're supposed to be good."

"Why won't you look at your new house?"

"What's the meaning of this house?"

"This is a little present, this house."

"In honor of what?"

"Panama."

"Oh, God, Panama. I found your suitcase from the wedding trip. We never unpacked it."

"What was in it?"

"Ammo."

"What?"

"Ammo."

"Anything else?"

"*Burke's Peerage*. Linen. A beer."

We crossed Stock Island and on Big Coppitt I studied the slow, wind-moving electric lights on a one-man used-car lot. The hospital sat to our left in the marl and mangroves. We were drinking fast to avoid the queer noise of eternity in the air.

The Land-Rover was all wound up at fifty. It bumped over channels on hidden bridges and at Boca Chica warplanes lifted into the distance. Then we had some good old-time darkness unrelinquished to the age. Through the window, warm, wet Florida smells and the unyielding kiss of tires on moist pavement.

"What else did we leave in Panama."

"Don't ask me."

"Catherine."

"Well, don't."

"Why shouldn't I?"

"We left everything."

"I don't believe that. Come on."

"We left it all."

At lower Sugarloaf, I pulled over. I got out and shone my flashlight in the tidal slough. It was still; the stars and planets shone on the surface.

"Used to be crabs here."

"What kind of crabs?"

"Blue crabs."

"Is that eating crabs?"

"The best. Sometimes they were soft-shelled. They looked the same as hard-shelled but I couldn't be sure enough to pick them up. I knew I'd get the misfit who'd kept his shell and he'd do a number on my hand."

Danny and the Juniors were on the radio, quiet and remote. The pavement stretched in front of the windshield. I turned to Miami Cuban radio and listened to Celia Cruz and watched the incursions of water glint along the road.

"Is the nation at war?" I asked.

"Not for some time. Don't you watch Walter Cronkite?"

"I don't go to the movies."

"Well, there's no war. There's an election."

"How're they doing?"

"Fine."

That made me feel good. I felt good all the way to the Chat-and-Chew on Summerland; and by Big Pine, it was time to turn out toward No Name. It became darker and the pines were tall and reaching and didn't look like they feared falling in the ocean or getting blown over. They were pines that dared to suggest that islands are misery where brave horsemen run off the earth and topple into the unknown.

There was darkness but there was still shade and we flashed by an old man in a white shirt standing by the road watching the stark, queer trees. Then the sky bent into the road and we were at the No Name Bridge. Catherine looked at the old man and then at me. Was it Jesse? I couldn't very well ask her.

I pulled over. You could see the stars in the water and the tide gathered against the pilings. I carried the sandwiches and Catherine closed her hands in front of her, as if something was happening. I dropped a pebble from the rail and it plunked like in a well, though it was sea water passing between islands.

"Going where?" Catherine asked.

"What?"

"The sea water."

"Was I talking out loud?"

"Yes."

"I don't know, from the Gulf to the Atlantic. From Gulf Shores to Atlantic View. From Gulf Rest to Atlantic-Aire." This was me, side-slipping. Catherine busted me.

"Why do you need to add those things? Whatever poetry is in you, you hate like everything."

"That's where the sea water was going."

"No it wasn't."

We walked to the middle of the bridge and found what little moving air there was. When I looked down at the water, it was the darkest part of the night. It showed silver against the abutments or you couldn't have seen it; it could have been the drop-off, the edge of the world.

"You know he's back."

"Who?"

"You must talk to him. You must settle that with yourself."

"He's dead."

"Do you believe that? You talked to him on the phone."

Oh, God, Oh ghosts, all on threads in the dark, not to be spoken to. Catherine, don't make me see this. There are stains, seeps, things you do not see. I had to look into the night; and sure enough, I was provided a skimmer bird, opening a brilliant seam in the water.

"Did you see that?" I asked.

"Yes, lovely."

"Hungry?"

"Sorry."

The old man in the white shirt was upon us before we heard him coming; we couldn't speak until he had passed on. Catherine stared at him again. I was afraid.

"You can't make everything up," Catherine said gently.

"Like what?"

"You can't make up that they're dead. And the others," she said, "they'll all turn up too."

"There's only one I want to see."

"Yeah, I know," she said. "Jesse James."

An outboard went under the bridge on a long white V and disappeared. Beyond the channel a light moved on the highway. The wake slapped under the bridge. Catherine peered at me and said, "I wonder who that old man was?"

"No way of knowing."

"He seemed to stare at everything. He was staring at me. He knew everything and he was staring."

She climbed up on the railing, teetering over the water, and I knew she was loaded from the piña coladas. I ate a crab-salad sandwich.

"You're going to fall off that and drown," I said.

"So what."

"Then where will you be?"

Catherine jumped. At first I saw her in the air, then she was gone in the blackness, and then she lit up in her silver splash and disappeared.

I ran across the bridge to the shore. I couldn't see anything and I broke my way along the mangroves down tide from the bridge and listened. The light through the leaves was like candle flames. I couldn't see anything but I could hear voices. I was all caught up inside my chest and I felt everything sweeping toward something where there was no light.

I kept going, watching the water, toward the voices. The mangroves stood up black on their roots, hermit crabs clinging underneath and rattling to the ground as I pushed through. Then there was a muddy indentation of the shore where the tide whispered past.

Catherine was lying there and the old man in the white shirt was arranging her hair like a sunburst in the mud. When he saw me, he stood up and moved away until his shirt smeared the dark. I bent over Catherine, her face pale between the black arrows of hair.

She said, "Are we alive?"

9

I dropped Catherine at her home. She never spoke again that night. Then I drove across the island to my place. There was something going on inside. I walked around very carefully, listening to mayhem in my house. I opened the door through the wall cautiously.

Inside, my dog cowered by the stack of plant pots, one eye swollen shut from a blow; and just beyond, Nylon Pinder was tipping over the furniture and flinging drawers across the room, kicking the bottoms out from under standing lamps and tearing up anything that would tear.

He turned when I came in and moved wide as his smile toward me and sent my teeth spinning through lamplight. It seemed an obvious extension of my beef with Peavey. But I asked him why he had hit the dog. This only reminded him and the grin became one of discovery. He headed for the dog and I headed for a tipped-over lamp. I picked up a piece of milk glass about the time he got to the dog and hit him in the side of the face with it.

He turned in astonishment and what there was was very much like the earlier smile; but it went back to his ear on one side and you could see teeth all the way.

"Run," I said. "You're bleeding to death."

The morning *Citizen* said that Nylon Pinder had taken a tumble and was in satisfactory condition in Memorial Hospital. Next, I would have to begin on Peavey before he began on me.

I was feeling somber. I was the subject of assaults and menaces, told that the dead were alive; and I was in love with a woman who didn't seem to care for anything except an evasion of the light that I understood but knew, as she did not know, to be poison. One false move and we'd all go under together.

I walked down to Duval Street and spent a quarter on a machine that analyzed my handwriting. I learned that I was given to emotional crescendos. I must have made some audible response because the proprietor of the arcade, a man so bald and so bearded as to suggest that his hair was on upside down, came up to me and glanced at my analysis card and asked me what I did. I told him I was a regimental musician at Vera Cruz. He asked what I was doing in Key West and I told him that my patent attorney, my allergy specialist, and the vicissitudes of my root canals urged a move.

There was a door at the back of the arcade that said "Adult Material." I passed through and played a dirty-movie machine with a fifty-cent piece. A fat girl came on the screen, undressed, and hit the deck. She retracted her legs as a naked man trotted toward her. Her bum was like a turret. The gentleman penetrated this valved protrusion with martial address until the fifty cents ran out. I sighed.

I said to the proprietor, "This is a perfect town for a quiet killing." There was no emotional crescendo in sight.

"I've got a few choice words for people like you," he said and I passed into the street with a peaceful smile. I walked to the Southernmost Point. A very old man and a very old woman were arguing.

She said, "I never *saw* so many oddballs. I want to get us out from under all these filthy people."

"I don't care about this," he said. "Did Robert fix the wind-up on the mower like I told him?"

"He best had!" she said with just as much vituperation as she'd displayed against the oddballs.

What I was doing was thinking and slowly circling back to Roxy's. I was nervous. I knew Peavey would be there. I didn't know whether to bring up Nylon Pinder; but I decided against it when I thought how cute Peavey was and how little chance there would be of his admitting such a connection.

Peavey behaved cordially. He was with Roxy among the grapefruits, trying to knock down a loner high in the tree with a bamboo pole. I was very slightly moved because the grapefruits were all Roxy owned up to caring about. Seeing Peavey try to get one down for her reconciled me to him a little.

Roxy said, "That Ruiz. I'm going to get a colored man, I swear I am."

"No," said Peavey, "you don't want one of those."

"I want a smart boogie."

He shook his head again. "If the colored people had any imagination . . . but they don't, do they? I mean, every urban area in the country is filled with pigeons—the Eurasian rock dove, that's what a pigeon *is*. And they could go out and gather all the pigeons they could eat, take them home, clean them, *pluck* them, and pop them in the rotisserie. Baste them liberally with butter and a bouquet of white wine and *herbes simple* . . . brown them to a turn! . . . and serve with a cold bottle of Montrachet. Mwah!" He kissed his fingers. "But they won't do this. There's a lack of imagination. I don't know what it is, protein deficiency, the gene pool, I just don't know. But I do fear this guy is little more than a monkey. I fear this very deeply. I fear monkey shows in the inner cities as well as right here in Key West. We already have to watch out for our lives with many of these apes owning Coupe De Villes, Smith and Wessons, and Godknowswhat. These are powerful devices and they have them."

Then Peavey looked right at me.

"How are you?" he asked.

"Fine," I retorted.

"Don't overdo a good thing," he said.

"You smell upset," I said.

"I'm not," he said.

"Good," I said. "But you don't smell right."

Catherine, my ballad to you goes like this. You can replace me but I can't let you go because I can't let you go I can't that's all I just can't. The night you sat on my Gibson Hummingbird I forgave you even though it was the last thing Johnny Horton ever touched I didn't care because it was you. That writer has a girlfriend too. She used to be Joe Cain's widow. He said she used to ride a train called the Hummingbird from Mobile to New Orleans. When he goes home, he's going to take her with him. I think she'll go. And how come you and me are always in pieces?

That night I dreamed again and again of the old man arranging Catherine's hair on the mud while the tide whispered past. Two dreams out of three he was faceless; in the third, he was my father.

"Hello—"

"This Nylon Pinder."

"Hello, Nylon."

"I'm home from the hospital."

"Right . . ."

"And feelin real good."

"Yes, Nylon."

"And you should think about that."

"Thank you, Nylon, I will."

I got off and reflected upon Nylon. I supposed

he was dangerous but he seemed merely pitiful, manipulating his voice and announcing his ominous return as per some TV show he'd seen. It is very very hard in this life to be a nincompoop. I called him back.

"Say, I'm having a party at the Casa Marina Saturday. Can you make it?"

"Oh," said Nylon, "I already *was* going to make it."

Nylon is very close, save for certain root, unpremeditated instincts, to what I spent a number of years enacting. I was a simple occupant, the man the anonymous senders of junk mail have in mind when they buy the stamp. And it was only my ability to see something in the accretion of toothpaste on unscrubbed counters, the signaling stain from plugged eaves troughs, the smell of myself in fear, as unattractive and profound as the funk of unloaded clothes hampers, that propelled me into the public nerve net with the ability to terrify with a smile or merely missing teeth. My affection for the ordinary, for Joe Blow in all his wonder, has deprived me of the power. But if the recoil doesn't kill me, if my affections don't kill me, I may laugh all the way to the bank; and without ever becoming The Occupant again, I could be happy. Not happy with a grin and the days flying by, but picking up the hours like shining stones. Meanwhile, it is sea level, incidents of torpor, and I know that I have been preceded in death. But if Catherine and I find a way to be happy together, we'll step aside when desolation roars past.

When I met my grandfather for the last time, he was riding an old singlefoot horse and carried his cane in a saddle scabbard. He looked at me for a long time, standing before him in my corduroys, T-shirt, and red tennis shoes; and said, *"Oh, what's the use?"*

Marcelline popped in.

"Two dudes outside want to know if you'll back them in the far-out tie-tack business."

"No."

She stepped outside and called, "No."

Then she came back in and rubbed up against me.

"Got time to feed it in?" she asked.

"No."

"Want to rob a crypt with my honey and me?"

"No, sir."

"He had to leave New Orleans. They used smear tactics against him."

"The term 'grave robber' doesn't sit well with people."

"They could of said 'breaking and entering.' If a person busts into a store front, they say 'B and E,' not store-front robbery. They called him a grave robber so it would go harder on him. He had to jump bail, no ifs, ands, or buts about it."

"I see your point," I said wanly.

"Anyhow, we located this crypt has this lieutenant from the pirate squadron in it, hundreds of years old. It could be damn near anything in there. We'll be in the cemetery tonight."

She darted through the wall into the blinding light.

I felt I had got used to Marcelline. She seemed

like a moron. I'm sure she's not. At this point, time had had that effect. I don't like anything time does, so I'm not sure why I'm buying this. But she did seem quite the little moron.

I waited until Marcelline was clear, then I went outside and got almost nine dollars from the wishing well. I don't know who got the impostor's silver dollars. I pushed my hands into my pockets and looked up the street at the cars under the palms, the lawns against the shattered sidewalk.

When Jesse James rode the trolley in St. Joseph, they could smell gunpowder in his clothing. I started crying again for the first time since the monkey bars.

On January 13, 1975, I got up from dinner at a small private bistro, popular with the professional psychodrama folks, called Fuck You. I am absolutely sure that I had a wonderful meal but ten minutes after I got up from the table I couldn't remember what I ate.

I had been dining with Jean-Luc Godard, who was a little down on his heels and looking for a new slant, in other words, me. He said, "It is simple, Chet. We return to Fuck You and ask the maitre d'." He couldn't remember what I ate either.

I said, "Nuts to that, Jean. I will just have to eat again. And in case you remember what I ate, I'd rather you didn't say."

"But aren't you full?"

"That's going to have to be my tough luck."

I had another large and this time disgusting meal at Luchow's, including a ghastly platter of

Black Forest mushrooms. All the while a hideous Bavarian orchestra in lederhosen blared at my table. Imagine my discomfort!

But: it kept happening for years to come, sometimes three meals in a row. Eventually it culminated in a very unfortunate episode with the mayor of New York.

Catherine said, "This business about Jesse James, I wish you'd stop. It makes my skin crawl."

"Why?"

"He's deader than a doornail."

"Wait a minute."

"Dead. And you know something? Nobody else has these troubles we do. I don't like this. I don't believe we ever needed your fame. I don't think I ever had to leave South Carolina—"

"We sought to be illustrious."

"I want to be happy."

"You said that."

"I want to be happy."

"Catherine—"

"I want to be happy."

"Jesse James was happy."

"He was trigger-happy."

"That's happy."

"I just want to be happy."

"Catherine, come on now."

"Make me happy." She was starting to sob.

"How?"

"Do it. Stay out of Panama. Please let us be happy."

"Happiness is just a guy named Joe," I said to lighten the atmosphere.

"Well then," she said through her teeth. "You and Joe stay the fuck out of Panama."

I stole a look at her through my terror of her authority, and through this vivid teeth-clenched fury, her face, lit by street lamps shining through the leaves of dead palms, seemed transcendent and fine, like the face of a legendary princess killed by lightning. I was lucky to have been in her life.

"Do I have to listen to this," I said gingerly and she slapped my face, one ringing blow, then idly stirred yet another piña colada while watching a little sloop look for a place to anchor. For all I knew, she could have been Jesse, a token of his power to inhabit my loved ones at will.

10

I HAD JUST RUN a lemon rind around the inside of my coffee cup, and I was staring at the awakening rummies on the icehouse loading dock, when Don sat down.

I said, "Beat it, Peewee."

"Just doing my job."

He was dressed in a suit this time, with the kind of three-button jacket and ill-fitting pants that used to be high with academics from nice families, so that a college kid could look up and say to himself, *That's no smart-ass big-city Jew, that's people.*

"I want my breakfast," I said. "I don't want to hear I molested an infant in Spokane at 3 a.m. when I thought I was sleeping."

"No, but you refused to speak to your father when he called."

"How would you know that if it were true?"

"Lineman's phone. Got alligator clips and I just plug into your wire."

"Uh huh."

"You told your father he had a wrong number."

"*Shut up! He's dead!*"

The fry cook turned around and stared but kept on scraping.

"And you bounced a check for five hundred thousand dollars."

I got up. "I don't need this."

"You wrote a sixty-thousand-dollar check for a conch house on Caroline. That bounced."

"*Check please.*"

The waitress quickly reached me a ticket. I slapped my empty pockets in panic. She couldn't keep her eyes off me.

"I got it," said Don and tossed the thirty cents onto the counter. "And *that* might be the last I can do for your memory. —I'm heading for the pay window."

Running on Dey Street, I slide on casuarina seeds and lose a shoe and bang my head and make blood where the cobbles come from under the tar. An old lady leans out from the balcony of the octagonal house, glances at the welding shop, jets snuff into the trees, and says, "You all right?"

There is a trigger that makes the day begin and all life end and it breaks like a glass rod. It lies at the middle of everything that breathes or dreams. It will bend and break, and when it breaks it is night.

I look up to tell her that I have hurt my head but noises even I can't make out pour from my mouth.

Two of them make a chair of their arms and they put me under the flashing light. One says his eyes are points and the other says Nylon's gone to appreciate this. I feel sleep coming but I'm not crying and it's okay because for once I'm not afraid of the ghosts.

"Jim," I said to my brother, "do me a favor. Show me how you died."

"What do you mean? You say Daddy's dead."

"He died in the Boston subway fire."

"*I* died the *day* of the Boston subway fire. You just slipped him in there too."

"Tell me."

"Not if you say Daddy is dead."

"Okay he's not dead."

"Say he's alive."

"I can't."

"Say it."

I said it and started to choke. Someone I couldn't see ran a finger into my mouth and pulled my tongue free. I vomited and for a moment lost Jim in the sailing shapes. But that lifted and it was sunny and he was there with the innocence I never had, still in his face; all the trust that let him be murdered by his life without humiliation.

"Everything went off and left me," Jim said.

They took me to Catherine's on my release. There was no bandage around my head, no bump, nothing. I had had a concussion and was supposed to lay low. I had few impressions except that my eyes had grown small, the worst had been wished on me, I had found something out from Jim, and I was among the living. My dog was missing.

"I don't know where she is," Catherine said.

"Well, we've got to find her." I told her to call the pound, tell them it was Deirdre, spots, white feet, missing. I was thinking of those men, their frayed nerves and the gas. There was no answer. I said run an ad. Catherine covered the mouthpiece.

"The paper wants to know what she answers to."

"She doesn't."

She uncovered the mouthpiece and said, "Spots is the main thing I guess." She hung up and came over. "Oh, darling, I love you. Get better. Stop being under such a strain."

"I can't seem to."

"Of course you can."

"Every time I try to relax, I start crying. I don't feel like a grown man that way."

"Where is it written you have to be a grown man?"

"All over the place."

"It's not."

I could hear a shrimper's diesel backing down at Brito's yard; and the vacuum-cleaner sound of the bus. Catherine watched me steadily. I covertly tried to see if her eyes would shift; they didn't.

"I looked at my new house," she said. "It was lovely."

"Oh, I'm glad."

"Very carefully made."

"Porch boards are sprung."

"That'll give us something to do."

"And I'd like a wooden grill around the foundations so that cats don't get under there and . . ."

". . . and fight."

"Yes, and fight under there all the time."

"Yes."

"They better find my dog. They don't find my dog I'm calling Jesse."

Catherine watched me, her eyes two stones in the mercury air.

Sometime later I awakened and Catherine was sleeping beside me, warmth radiating from her brown back, and I laid my face in the channel between her shoulder blades and pulled her thick curly hair around her neck so that I could look at the telegraph wires in the window. Warm moist air moved in a gentle mass over us; and across the way, a radio played a giddy weather report for the tourists. In the bottom of the window, laundry floated into my view. I felt like sailing with my love, feeling the centerboard hum in the wooden hull, the shapes of islands vault past our daydreams.

That or reviewing my life; but a good bit too much life reviewing has gone on already. The only wisdom it produces is the resolution to not do any further reviewing. My nose itched and I ground it against Catherine's spine. She stirred and curved her bottom up against me; and then again, and then we were sleepily making love. When we were done, she turned and put her arms around me and her face against my chest and said, "Oh, darling, get well."

The statement seemed to come from a very far place within her. I didn't know exactly what she meant by it; but I felt, with great strength, that I wanted to give that to her. I wanted to get well. I just didn't know what that was. If there was a fear, it was that I had *never* known; that I had been strikingly not well from the start; that my ticket to ride, such as it was, was based on the vividness of disease; and that I was paying for everyone else.

My first instinct was that a social life depended simply upon giving people what they wanted. So, I called Peavey, as a kind of test case.

I told him that I had finally understood that marriage was what Roxy wanted and that I therefore endorsed that view and would see Roxy that very day to make myself clear.

"Why, that's very nice."

"I am going to try to stop interfering," I said.

"I think you should."

"I am going to attempt to be normal," I said, "eat regularly, see some motion pictures, and take in the hot spots on weekends."

"Right . . ."

"And anyway, that's all."

"Well, that's very nice. And look here, I'd like to return the favor. I got a line on your dog. I'll have Nylon Pinder drop it by."

"Say," I said, "thanks a lot. I appreciate that. Nylon been feeding her pretty good?"

"Not too bad. Not too damn bad."

"Well, that's good, isn't it?"

"A house pet should have special care," Peavey said.

"Well," I said, "I'll be talking to you."

"Real good, and thanks!"

Catherine was looking at me.

"I'm trying," I explained. It was quiet.

She said, "You're the original snowball in hell." She was shaking all over.

11

MY UNCLE PAT was in his yard on a step-ladder, out in the middle of the yard, wiring a creeper to a freestanding trellis. He was in some aerial relationship to the trellis, as though he, on his ladder, were feeding it like a tall bird.

"Pat, Roxy wants to get married."

"I don't care a thing about it."

"I'm making my party at the Casa Marina a wedding party. But she wants to know if you'll come."

"I couldn't say, Chet." A bead of sweat fell from the tip of Pat's nose sixteen feet to the ground.

"It's going to be dressy as hell, Pat. And there'd, you know, be a ceremony."

"But would I figure?"

"You'd have to work that out with Roxy."

"It'd be good to have something other than Peavey's henchmen and their trashy girlfriends."

"That's why I thought you might stand up for Roxy."

"Can I dress?"

I hesitated, but not for long. Pat lived to dress up. It was the key to his attending. I said sure. He got happy quick and the ladder started over. He reached and embraced the trellis. They went down together in parallel. In the descending arc, I could see his happy eyes.

"I'm okay," he said.

"The plant's shot," I said, looking at the turmoil of vines.

"I don't have a green thumb," he said. His mind was already on the wedding, his eyes glowing with yet unseen ceremony. I myself thought of the wedding, the orchestra, Catherine, semi-familiar faces, a warm and swollen ocean beaded with the lights of ships. I helped Pat to his feet, lost in happiness. I knocked loose dirt from his getup. "You're a good uncle," I told him, remembering the crazy angles of my father's roof.

"If I could quit cruising," he said. "People talk."

Waiting in front of my house was a familiar man in safari clothes. His hair was slicked straight back without a part and he was chewing a cheroot.

"You are Ramón Condor," I said, "star of *The Reluctant Gaucho*."

"The keys."

"?"

"The check bounced on the Land-Rover. Get me the keys."

"They're in it."

He walked over to the car.

"This was a go-anywhere vehicle," he said, "now it's nothing but a repo."

"I'm sorry."

"You're a bald-ass liar and your checks are bum."

"I knew only confusion."

He was halfway in the car and he got out again. He flicked away the cheroot and cinched up his sa-fari coat. "*You knew only confusion . . .*" He started at me. There are those who despise my flair for lan-guage.

I saw another smack coming and I lowered my head between my shoulders for protection, simul-taneously turning my false-tooth-filled mouth to one side. But then when he got to me, I reflexively popped him in the side of the head and he sat down.

"This whole deal is getting highly Chinese," he said.

"Don't be coming at me like that."

"I oughta leave you for the birds."

"You'll have to get to your feet first."

"Nylon said, 'Let me collect that for you,' but me, I had to be big."

"Nylon hasn't been doing so good either."

"But if I hadn't had to be big, it would of been him instead of me. Now look. God damn polished cotton's worth its weight in gold. One knee's done for and the thing is an outfit, not just pants and a jacket. And a tough one to come by."

"They do reweaving down off Simonton Street."

"I did it. I have to live with it." He got in the Land-Rover and left.

"Where's he going in the Buick," Catherine asked.

I turned around. "Where did you come from?"

"Kiss me hard."

I held her.

"I just thought today, maybe I can stand it. You're out of the question but today I thought, it won't kill me."

"I never said that," I said. "I never said it would kill you."

I looked at her and she was glowing. She had evidently had some kind of moment with herself. I was holding it away. It seemed as if she was coming back or going to try and I didn't want to distort it; if I could just hold on to one place for her to come back to. She would do that for me. And why in hell couldn't I do that for her?

We walked around to the beach and Marcelline was there, sitting on a Ramada Inn towel and reading pornography. I had my arm around Catherine's waist when Marcelline commenced an excerpt; it was gruesome filth. She laughed, then stopped and looked up. "What's the matter?" she asked.

"I mean, I'm sorry," she said.

"Look," she said, getting up and folding her towel, "no salesman will call at your door."

She left.

"Huh," I said.

"Gee," said Catherine.

Then Marcelline was back and she was throwing rocks at us. "It's no call to do me like some doormat!" she shouted.

"Lay off the speed, Marcelline," Catherine said, "this always happens. It's venom . . . *put down those rocks.*" Marcelline vanished again, weeping this time. "It's venom, I tell you. Monday she's blowing one boyfriend in his sports car and by Wednesday she's cutting her wrists in another's apartment because he says he doesn't love her. Then by the time she gets back to the blowjob in the sports car, it's on holiday in Europe and Marcelline's standing there wondering why she's always holding the bag. One minute you're holding the bag, the next you *are* the bag."

"This is your version?"

"This is it, this is *la vie en rose*."

"Do you think it's possible for a little romance?"

"I seriously doubt it. It's like eating gravel."

Even in the sun, all the world seems to contain a hollow wailing moan, long and drawn out, as though purgatory understood the meaning of not knowing what was next.

"I love you so," said Catherine. "Whatever's missing in the world, I'm doing my part."

We passed down the purlieus of Duval Street, past vile restaurants addressed "Rue Duval." On the steps of St. Paul's Church, a pigeon worked its way diagonally below the feet of two elderly gentlemen, factional members of a Long Island exodus.

"We could have had such a damned good time together," I heard one say.

"Yes," replied the one in the bonnet, "isn't it pretty to think so."

"Now," said the former, "I'm heading home to put things by."

"Want to hear some poetry, Catherine?"

"Like what?"

"Sappho or Dylan Thomas?"

"You don't know any Sappho unless Marcelline told you."

"The fuck I don't."

"She better not be reading your ass poems."

I gave her my favorite Sappho. *"Someone, I tell you, will remember us. We are oppressed by fears of oblivion, yet are always saved by the judgment of good men."*

"I didn't think you knew one."

"I don't love Sappho as an excuse for eating pussy," I said. "Now, let me tell you the Dylan Thomas poem I like."

"None of the drunken slobber poems," she said.

"I'll tell you one that means the most to me: *A process blows the moon into the sun, pulls down the shabby curtains of the skin; and the heart gives up its dead."*

"Why is that one important to you?"

"I read it at my father's funeral."

"Your father didn't die, fuckface."

"Don't tell me that an event I know by heart didn't happen. I was the third mourner from the left in the funeral party and don't call me fuckface."

"That was your mother's funeral. You showed me the picture. She did die."

"My father died in the Boston subway fire!"

"Your father has never been in Boston! I asked him!"

We went into Fitzgerald's for a drink. The waitresses were stuffing rugs under the lid of the piano. When one came we ordered Stolichnaya and limes. My ears were ringing.

"What are you doing to that piano?"

"The guy we hired is good but he's too loud. He's a spade."

"That makes him too loud?"

"No, he happens to be an Afro-American person. I thought I'd mention that."

When she came back with the drinks, I said, "Those rugs are going to keep it from playing at all."

"It's worth a try."

"I think you're showing real aggression toward this musician."

"Leave her alone, Chet," said Catherine.

"We *love* him. He teaches all the ofay waitresses how to get down, and we do his charts and balance his aura."

"I see."

"Three dollars."

Catherine paid. I was on the humble, having mislaid my wallet. People were staring into the bar from outside. I let no one catch my eye. All they want are loans.

"Let's take a sink or swim approach," said Catherine.

"A little idle laughter or something?"

"Yeah, or something. We're getting morbid or something."

"Or something."

"How do you feel you're doing on your memory?"

"I'm avoiding that gumshoe like the plague. He's been dogging my heels, following me into restaurants with his shitsucker showdowns."

"I just wish out of respect for my investment you'd take the time to let him tell you what you've been doing."

"Catherine, why do we have to talk about him now?"

"He's looking at you."

I glanced up and sure as hell.

"What are you trying to do to my mind?" I inquired.

"Restore the original luster."

"Well, don't."

A member of Jorge Cruz's orchestra sat at the bar with an uncased yellow saxophone propped next to him, reminding me of my commitment at the Casa Marina. He ordered two shots of Mount Gay Eclipse and began to hum a nervous salsa tune while spying on me in the mirror. With everyone watching me, I began to think of the writer, the one who quit everything to go home so Joe Cain's widow could show him what was what. I could have gone with him and made a cowboy of myself or merely lived in a way that Jesse James would have understood, or even my grandfather with a cane in his scabbard and his

Lucky Strikes and his board-and-batten barn in Excelsior Springs with its lunatic memories of upside-down border fighters.

I could, in any case, restore myself in the glades I'd loved as a boy, hunting turtles and smelling gunpowder from my .22 instead of trotting the burnt-out nerves of the nation like an adenoidal Basenji. I could stop lying and try to improve my memory without being an utter fool about it.

Catherine took me to a house on Lopez Lane to carry a lamp home for her. We entered in back beside the cistern under the dogwood lintel and found ten people concluding a coke deal. "It's only me," sang Catherine and the deal went on, with a young scientist on a three-beam scale trying to break a little boulder into quarter ounces. I commenced feeling the strain. The subject of the deal was a normal-looking young businessman given away only by half-mast eyes. There was a very tiny girl at the table and she chopped one little nugget on a piece of marble. The businessman rolled a crisp fifty-dollar bill and the girl separated the blow into rails. Ceremoniously the marble slab went round the table, the businessman first, passing his rolled bill, and when it came back to him, the fifty had turned into a one. When Catherine came back into the room with her standing lamp, the businessman was on his feet shouting, "Fuck this noise the deal is off!" At which point the tiny girl produced the fifty and indignantly demanded to know where her one went to. "It's interest on my fifty," said the businessman. I put the lamp over my shoulder, swallowed my spit, and headed for Catherine's house.

"I was shocked when we went in there and saw what was going on," said Catherine. "But you stood tall in the face of all that coke." She was proud of me.

Once inside Catherine's house, she reached out, taking me by the front of my shirt. "Let me help you with your little things," she said and pulled the shirt violently open, shooting buttons around the room. I reached up and pulled the bead chain and saw the shadows of the fan race against the walls. Star holes appeared in my brain pan. I looked down the front of her Cuban blouse and saw a nipple aiming in space with agonizing delicacy. I realized that the crew of the cucumber boat at Mallory dock had been in a position to spot these glands when we had walked— see, I can remember this—and discussed without raving our own lives together in the rooms and corridors of big-city hotels.

From the bedroom I heard a gruff voice, "Oral love, not that! I'm no shootist!" Catherine jerked open the door and there was Marcelline with the agent, that sight, engaged in a blur of manual intercourse. She shut the door again.

"Your place," she said. When we opened the door to go out, there was an intelligent-looking young man poising his hand to knock. "Go to it," said Catherine to him, "they've got the jump on you though." I had to race to keep up. The breeze poured into my buttonless shirt. "That was the grave robber," said Catherine. "He had a synthesizer fellowship at Juilliard."

"He looks it."

"Give me any other century," she replied. She

insisted on making two stops: one to buy an album called *Great Waltzes of the World* and another for six bottles of Evian mineral water. When we got to my place, we put on the record and danced until we polished off the mineral water. The dog watched the prom from the sunny patio. Playing cards of afternoon light from the kitchen window crawled across the floor until my father's picture lit up on the wall and I screamed holy murder.

"I'm getting out of here."

"Sit down," said Catherine.

"Bugger that, my ears are ringing."

"Just calm down, Chet, please."

"My father led a long and heroic life at sea and died ironically in a tunnel under the city of Boston instead of at the helm of a schooner as he should have. It upsets me to see his likeness."

"Chet, please listen to me quietly. Your father is a happy man from Bunkerville, Ohio, who has made a fortune packaging snack foods. He is here in Key West. He wants to see you."

"He was always calling my bluff. He personally manufactured all the small, fine instruments necessary for giving my self-esteem back to the Indians. But he was a durable man of the high seas and it kills me he uh died of uh smoke inhalation."

"No high seas, no death. Happy snack-food packager."

"Nuts."

"True."

"Uh-uh, nuts. Can we go in there?"

"You're not getting off that way. I'm not interested in going to bed with you five minutes after you're screaming at a framed portrait."

"*Do I have to be attractive twenty-four hours a day?*"

"*You have to be attractive once in a while.*"

"Oh, brother."

"Go for a walk. Calm down. And when you get back, I'll be waiting for you. I'll love you and hold you and kiss your eyelids. But I'm learning that I can't make you better."

I knew she would keep her word. So I went outside to collate these mysteries into a uniform package I could live with. This necromancy of Catherine's in attempting to bring the dead to life was out of the question. I had to decide why she wanted to lie to me about my father. Then I lost control of my feet and found myself speeding along the hedges, shouting, "Coming through!" whenever a knot of pedestrians ambled into my way. Like a heartsick housewife on a shopping spree, I thought an interesting acquisition would divert me from my pinwheeling insides and flying feet. Therefore, on Galveston Lane, I made arrangements to purchase a parrot which said Jesus, Mary, Joseph at the trilling of a bell, the sight of a monstrance or a cracker. We discussed wampum but the Cuban gentilhomme who owned the parrot wanted, I thought, in excess of its real value. I attempted to seize the parrot, having placed an amount equal to the parrot's real value upon the sideboard. But I was badly bitten by the parrot itself and obliged to beat a hasty retreat.

I was jumped by photographers in front of Bahama Mama's, and while a stenographer wrote frantically, I recited my Act of Contrition, genuflecting with enough sincerity that my knee could be heard against the sidewalk a hundred feet away. A photographer leaned in for a close-up and a tourist who had been staring at me, a middle-aged man in a LaCoste shirt, slapped the camera to the street and said to the photographer, "Leave him alone, you god damned ghoul." Once more my flying feet had me soaring down the island. I found I could knife sideways through streaming traffic without harm and even the shriek of brakes and horns seemed very far away. I could set my nose on the point of a cloud and run navigating the blocks of houses on Whitehead Street until my lungs caught fire and I had to lie down in front of the barbershop. Two men came out in their aprons, vividly black West Indians, and asked me what I was going to do now.

"Lie here get my wind."

"Need'ny hep?"

"Nope."

They went back in to finish their haircuts. I watched the movements of diverted feet as they passed my face until I had my breath. I sat up on my haunches until I could rise with some dignity and angle toward the Casa Marina. Electricity was running up my swollen arches and my bones felt translucent as I fled toward Catherine in subaqueous strides, eyes hanging low in their sockets and teeth vibrating very slightly against each other.

More than anyone else, pedestrians and out-of-towners are assailed by the forces of evil. Moving through these hopeless ones, I knew that they would have to go some to help me at all. Everybody has a rough time getting what they come for. The real cowboys are all in drugstores; these people got hung up in the rigging.

As soon as I got to the house, I could see Mrs. Dean carrying a Portuguese man-of-war to the ocean on a stick. Last fall her Chow ate one and went to his reward making unearthly noises at both ends. She turned her eyes slowly toward me.

Catherine said, "I can't rise above it. I can't stand it."

"May I come in?"

"God, what happened to your head?"

"I was attempting to purchase a beautiful green parrot."

"What happened to your finger?"

"I fell. No one came to me. I curse this nation."

"You what?"

"I curse this nation. Can you imagine the time I'm having?"

We went inside. I noted the air of mildew. I am a Floridian and I accept the mildew.

The first thing I told Catherine was that I was glad the marine biologist knocked his eye out, the one he looked through the microscope with, glad, the rotten one-eyed shitsucking wage ape.

No reply. I was being indulged. O God, this isn't funny and only the sonorous, vacant sea gave me any sense of truth, truth in the sense of what was in store: circulating minerals.

Then I felt horrid again and I wanted a family with Catherine. I wanted us to want the same thing with no hideous discussions of our rights and obligations. I would be Papa Bear and there would be peace, peace in the valley for . . . for me. And over the chimney, the shimmer of smokeless fuel. There would be rabbits on the lawn in the evening. And Jesse's saddle horse would be in the tie stall with the morning light on his shining coat.

"What is this?"

"A compress. You've got an egg on your forehead. Can't you hit something besides your head? And look at these."

She showed me Roxy's wedding invitations. The party at the Casa Marina was mentioned. I stared at the raised engraving and felt the weight in my pocket. "What's that noise?" I said.

"The trash collector."

"Jesus, it seems right in the room."

"Give me the gun."

"It's mine."

"Give it to me."

I handed it over.

"Let me ask you something. Would you consider seeing a psychiatrist?"

"Not at all."

"Why?"

"They are disease profiteers."

"You need help."

"I'm doing fine."

"As what?"

"An angler on the sea of God's mysteries."

Catherine fed the dog, turning the can in a patented opener while Deirdre ran around on her hind legs like an exotic dancer. More and more, the gentle movements of the sea had come to sound like hoofbeats. I touched my compress and licked the beak hole in my forefinger. There was a chameleon on the screen puffing his vermilion throat against the wire.

Then Catherine found my rosary in the margarine tub: "What the fuck is this?"

"Only at night."

"What?"

"For sleepless nights. Beads, vodka, and walking the dog."

"Have you gone down to the pier?"

"No."

"Your father's boat is anchored there."

"Here we go."

"Here *you* go. You ought to have a look. Lot of money in snack-food packaging, by all appearances."

"Why do you say that?"

"Because *that* is how the boat was paid for and it's about a city block long. Look and see."

I thought that I would try to detail as much of this vapid lie as I could. I laid my plans as I slept on the sea-grass rug. When I awoke, Catherine was gone. There was a salad made for me in the icebox and a loaf of Cuban bread.

I put on my bathing suit and walked along the beach toward the pier. I made my way around a restaurant whose tables stood empty, legs plunged in sand, unused paper napkins fluttering in an ocean breeze. I had to wade around a piney promontory before I could see the boat. She was anchored about a quarter mile offshore, bow to the southeast trades. This was not the first time I'd been beset by impostors.

I could tell she was white though it was dark, and the portholes glowed warmly. I slipped into the water and began to swim. I don't know how long it took. I was not in the best of shape and I was exhausted by the curious morning running across our island town. But I got to the boat, touching its towering bow and holding myself for a rest. Then I let the tide carry me along the hull, through the panels of yellow light, my fingertips gliding over the rough barnacles at the waterline. From somewhere above the rail, I could hear Jesse's voice; he spoke angrily of the eating habits of Americans, claiming they never knew what they wanted. I knew what I wanted.

When I got to the stern, I knew for the first time how deep Catherine's scheming against my sanity had become. Above my head, in enormous brass letters, it said: S.S. SNACK. And directly over the transom, the man I'd first thought I'd heard speaking stood. It was the old man on No Name Key whom I had discovered arranging Catherine's hair on the mud. He had the cane from my grandfather's scabbard and he worked it between his two hands as he stared down, down, at me, suspended in a warm ocean. I released my hold on the rudder and let the tide carry me into darkness.

12

I STAYED IN BED a very long time. I was not alone. I was very thirsty and drank glass after glass of flat Key West tap water. Thanks to Don. Don filled the glasses from a yellow plastic pitcher as he told me where I had been and what I had been doing. Then an ice cube jammed the spigot and Don, while trying to refill my glass, slopped about a half quart through the top of one of his mesh two-tones.

"That's the first thing you've done for which you should have been paid," I said aggressively. "Now let me tell you something. I don't care what I've been doing or whether it was right or wrong because it will all come out in the wash—" Don opened his wallet and let the credit cards plummet from his hand in their accordion plastic enclosure.

"Take these. You're broke. You can ruin my credit. My signature is easy to forge. But take these and use up my money until you're satisfied I'm not in it for the money."

"What are you in it for?"

"Memory. It's the only thing that keeps us from being murderers."

"Well, I don't have one."

"I want to rebuild it."

"I don't want it back."

"You *must* have it back."

"Oh, no you don't."

"What do you mean?"

"Telling me god damn you that I can't proceed without knowing where I've been. Don't pull that old malarkey on me. Where you from anyway? Penciltucky? You god damn spy. Here I am to start with, half frozen, from trying to pay a god damned visit to a very important American citizen—"

"Who's that?"

"Who's what?"

"This very important American citizen."

"C'mon. You know who it is."

"I want to see if you have the balls to tell me."

"I can tell you."

"Well, tell me."

"Who I went to see?"

"Yeah, who."

"Jesse James."

"Jesse James has been dead for a century, mister. He was shot by Bob Ford whilst attempting to hang a picture."

"Never happened."

"I'm telling you—"

I had to shout. *"Bob Ford never got it done."* I calmed myself. "A picture of what?" I then asked.

"What d'you mean?"

"Jesse James was hanging a picture of what?"

"A landscape. Let's say a landacape of Missouri."

"Which would be what?" Jesse owned one picture : a photograph of his horse, Stonewall Jackson.

"Thickets."

"Thickets." I thought that this was a paltry fabrication.

"You heard me."

"Well, I say he never got shot by Bob Ford."

"You want to get smacked? Do you know how ugly it is not to give in to someone trying to save you?"

"No." I saw the skinny detective would hit me. He wasn't man enough for some red-blooded despair.

Jesse, forgive them, for they know not what they do.

I don't think I've ever mentioned my first meeting with Catherine. Do I start on this because the end is in sight? I couldn't face that; and, in fact, a certain giddy courage accompanies my ever raising the question at all. I don't think I could survive with less than the hope of a long life under American skies, with Catherine. At the same time, I know that it's been one crisis after another. But, what of it. We met in a San Francisco pet shop where I had boarded my toucan. The toucan had been mistakenly sold;

and since the store smelled of monkey droppings, I accused the manager of incompetence. Catherine watched from a distance, and when our exchange became rather cruel, she began releasing animals; first the gerbils, and working her way up to the primates. She hated meanness and by the time she had averted what had every chance of becoming an ugly fight, there were a number of fanciful creatures, tropical and otherwise, running out the door to disappear among the busy feet of pedestrians. "This," thought I to myself, "is my kind of girl."

There were bills to be paid, after which we adjourned to a Japanese-style restaurant which served Serbo-Croatian food in addition to raw fish and a startling marshmallow salad that was absolutely gratis to anyone who came through the door and braved the wilderness of bentwood coat racks in the foyer. Even there, I was not oblivious to certain family glories of mine, the sound of horses in the underbrush—perhaps "thickets" is *not* the wrong word— gunpowder in percussion Colts, tired men in their hangouts, haunted Missouri barns.

Over the top of my salad, I could see faces pressed to the glass amid Japanese lettering.

"What do they want from you?" asked Catherine.

"I don't know. But my job is to make them think they're going to get it."

She looked at me; you know how—long and assessing, ending with a sudden grin. I want to isolate this, the sudden smile, emerging as it does in Catherine as—what?—well, as a sunburst, from deep thought. Similarly, when after puzzling over some confusion, Catherine says no, it is as sudden and fatal as the sunburst smile. It is over. Do you see? Over.

Then we went and hung around the Richmond–San Rafael bridge. I stared ruefully at Alcatraz while Catherine wrote our names on the abutment, in a heart, with a chalky stone, scratching away and talking about the South and the poor complexions of San Francisco while I, as usual, talked about the dead and near-dead. Catherine, strong and living, had thrown herself at my feet. I couldn't shut up.

I had at that time a bodyguard who had had a distinguished career as a U.S. Marshal in Portland and Northern California. His name was Roy Jay Llewelyn and he had survived many shootouts in Federal Service. He had also sent many people to Alcatraz, and as Catherine and I played, he gazed serenely at its impregnable shape.

Roy knew many other hired guns in the area, some U.S. Marshals, and they were a little society of men who showed each other their bullet holes. Later, when Marcelline spoke of triggermen, I thought of Roy.

Roy took Catherine and me to the dump at south San Francisco. The triggermen were there, car lights trained on a hill of rubbish, shooting rats. On the hoods of their cars were supertuned Pachmayr combat pistols. The hill was ignited like a movie screen, and back in the dark, the cigarettes of gunslingers glowed over the sound of AM car radios. Now and then, a voice: "There's a damn goblin, Roy." A rat would creep through the glare of illegal hot car lights—quartz iodide shimmer on wet fur—and Roy

Jay Llewelyn would drop into position and let the goblin have it. As night sank in, hungry rats threw caution to the winds while Catherine and I crawled into the back seat of Roy's triple-tone Oldsmobile. Gently, I undressed Catherine for the first time while the younger gun hands crowded around Roy. We made love for a long while as the automatics popped and rat parts flew among the rubbish. San Francisco then had been an earlier song, a song of Alcatraz, pet stores, Japanese-Croatian restaurants, gunmen, and rat gore. Love affairs have begun more prettily; but that was the only one we got. I was a star and couldn't just walk around.

Catherine had been living for a year and a half on three Maxwell House coffee cans of inherited jewelry. She was so frugal then that there were, when I met her, still two cans left, including the one that contained her great-aunt Catherine's emerald bracelet, bought for her by her husband when he commanded a ship for the Navy in China.

I swept Catherine off her feet to the Sherry-Netherland Hotel, years before rich rock-and-roll fascists took it over. At that time, it was a hotel where the staff specialized in memorizing faces just to tell you how good it was to see you again.

I was making a tremendous living demonstrating, with the aplomb of a Fuller Brush salesman, all the nightmares, all the loathsome, toppling states of mind, all the evil things that go on behind closed eyes. When I crawled out of the elephant's ass, it was widely felt I'd gone too far; and when I puked on the mayor, that was it, I was through. I went home to Key West and voted for Carter.

We set a room service record.

I would send out for little things. A single pack of Salem Longs. Trifles. We had much sex, even while on the phone; or during Ed McMahon dog-food commercials, where a spaniel would choose between two bowls. When Catherine took her chair into the bathroom to play with the taps, I knew we'd been in the hotel too long. The message light was flashing on the phone. There were huge blue grapes soaking the morning *New York Times*. I called to check out. News of what I'd done to—or, I should say, *on*—the mayor had hit the hotel. The staff stared at me. I said the mayor would soon be writing spy novels in prison like other government felons; but I had little conviction. They didn't like me and they didn't think I was funny.

At La Guardia, I wore dark glasses and ate about a pound of Oreo cookies, after which I could have really nailed the mayor, but I thought, "Why cry over spilt milk?"

Nighttime 707 Commuter to Miami: little reading lights ignited the disembodied arms in rows in front of me, arms which listlessly flipped airline magazines, or held cigarettes to stream smoke into the cones of light now and then swept aside by the air current behind a hurrying stewardess. All of us passengers were torn from our origins. Red and green lights shimmered on riveted aluminum wings and beneath us my little America, my baby madhouse, deployed towns and farms and cities against the icy ruinous transept of time and the awful thing which awaits it.

Catherine and I swallowed cocktails from the

cart, though we seldom had the correct change and
drew ugly glances from the stewardesses. I felt that
my hands and feet were swelling up and that the
pilot had falsified the cabin pressure. I felt too that
having to go up and down the aisle at night, to put
up with incorrect change and the flight crew's demand for snacks, was infuriating the stewardesses
and that any minute an atrocity directed at the
sheeplike passengers with their magazines could
break out. Catherine and I were in tough shape men-
tally; and we had started to fear the stewardesses.
As though to throw fat on the fire, they began to
gather in the tail of the plane, to ignore the call buttons and to block the toilet. My stomach was full of
butterflies and when I saw an old man gesture helplessly to a stewardess as she shot to the tail, I felt I
had to do something for us all. I unfastened my
seat belt, catching Catherine's alarmed glance, and
started aft. I thought as I glided above the passengers that I saw their hopes of something better wing-
ing to me.

The stewardesses glowered toward my approach.
They were in a little group. There were sandwich
wrappers and styrofoam. An aluminum door was ajar
behind them and toilet light flooded forth. They had
more food than we did. They seemed to glance at
one blonde, a Grace Kelly type with a Bic crossways
in her tunic. I was afraid.

When I reached them, I said, "There's an old
man who needs a glass of water. Can you help?"

The blonde stared through me. Then she
reached up and touched a switch. Over three hundred passengers, RETURN TO SEAT appeared in lights.

"Hit it," said the blonde.

"I wonder if I—"

"Can't you read?"

"The old man needs—"

"I don't care what he needs. We are entering turbulence. Return to your seat and extinguish all smoking materials." Then she added something which signaled the beginning of my understanding that the end of my glory was at hand. "You rotten pervert," she said. "Blowing your cookies all over the mayor of New York."

Zut alors! I am in arrears with everyone; else why are they all explaining the sky is blue or yesterday I ate breakfast twice? *Why*? Someone said, "Two plus two equals four is a piece of insolence." And these simpletons think I shall accept their reports at face value! Not possible; a thousand times no.

I'm not complaining. If people accept me as I am, that is, fallen from a high place, and don't assume that I am in despair and require that actuality be described to me, why then a happy liaison of spirits is always a possibility. But not if we are doing ABCs on the state of reality.

Enough of this. The marriage of my aunt, Roxanna Hunnicutt, impends. I must touch base with the orchestra.

But before I do, I would like to note that I, screw loose and fancy free, know certain things, that I am crazy like a fox. I know that Jesse robbed and killed and that he was lonely. I know he was left behind, left for dead. But I know he rose again from the dead. At the same time as these issues ring, I know that I must touch base with the orchestra.

As to this orchestra, I am an admirer; at the same time, I know better. I came of age like everyone else, wearing out copies of *Tupelo Honey*, feeling richly gloomy. Now in Los Angeles, Jackson Browne and the Eagles nurse everybody's bruises, and Mick Jagger, the tired old hag, says the Rolling Stones are the best punk band in the world. It's desperate. I prefer Jorge Cruz playing for endless Cuban weddings in Key West, the only city in America where you can buy novelty condoms in the municipal airport, and where the star of *The Dog Ate The Part We Didn't Like* can have a little peace.

The first thing Jorge said was, "I wait and I wait and you never get back to me."

"I had an egg on my head."

"I wait and I wait."

"Egg."

"I see the egg in the paper. I see your discharge from Florida Keys Memorial. Still I wait."

"Will you play for our family?"

"On one condition."

"Which is?"

"That the weeds are cut down at the Casa Marina so that my orchestra is not driven crazy with chiggers."

"It's a deal."

"You hurt my feelings when you didn't call. I thought it was my music."

"I neglected you. Accept my apologies."

"But I will, of course."

I let go of Jorge's handlebars. He rolled up
Lopez Lane and disappeared behind a car body. The
haze from City Electric brought its air of extraordi-
nary romance. Each filling station seemed like a
cheerful island with the bright pumps standing
bravely in the tropical smoke. Through the open
doorways of old homes came the anomalous ring of
cash registers or piping television serials. I was transfixed by a beauty beyond the hideous. My heart was
a song. Nothing hugs the road like a garbage truck.

I am enclosed in here, in my reflecto Ray-Bans.
Look at me and what do you see? Yourself.

Peavey is in his office. I'm relieved that he's out
of Roxy's Florida room with that girl, though I see
her behind the water cooler, huge bubbles rising
through her visage. She's changing a column of those
little one-swallow paper cups. She looks up at me
and for an instant a bubble enlarges her left eye to
the size of a melon.

I wave and she turns to Peavey, who's turned to
me.

"Counselor," I say.

"Chet."

"What's the word?"

"Beats me, Bubba."

"The hell you say." I grin.

"What can I do you for?"

"I got Jorge Cruz lined up."

"Fabulous."

"Tell you though, the guy laid a condition on
me. He wants the weeds down."

"We'll get them down but not because he said
so."

"Who do I call?"

"Southernmost Lawn. They got a big Weed Eater, go right through that junk. Got four Bahamians with grass whips. Put the place right in shape."

"There are a lot of cats in that deep grass," I say, starting to lose it already. Peavey fixes me and raises a Benson and Hedges to his lips.

"Well, they're going to have to get out."

"That's the heck of it," I say. Peavey knows I'm going down for the count. Might just as well face that.

"You seen that boat off White Street pier?"

I start around the desk and he says, "*Get out.*"

"Relax," I tell him. "This is no clambake and you are among friends."

I left Peavey balling the jack with bubblehead and all the lights on his phone shining like a southern constellation.

I stopped to see my uncle Pat. He used to be in American Intelligence and he has a tremendous amount of stuff from the Germans, including a phonograph and a stack of Nazi 78's, which he often plays while working. Pat's practice has gotten to where there's no need of an office. He works on the dining-room table listening to Nazi songs—he's not a Nazi—adding codicils and revising bills of grievance which he sometimes circulates free of charge. I told him two o'clock Sunday; no dresses. Pat wasn't making any promises. Also, and I can't be emphatic enough about this, he's no Nazi.

And then—then!—it was raining. Rain in Cayo Hueso can be a rare thing, as you streak over the cracked sidewalk under the awning of trees, a curtain of translucent rain, the endless hiss of traffic. The watery green leaves turn up and the dust on the Spanish limes rinses down till their dark, vivid forms stand out in their own clouds of green. I step to the left and the cloud water, the ocean rain, goes straight to my skin and I picture that my own form is as vivid in this fatigue shirt and jeans and Sonia sandals as a Spanish lime tree, soaking energy from the rain and getting ready to drop seeds on those roofs until everyone inside is crazy from not sleeping. Rain is one thing that will make you feel you can go on.

Roxy is being fitted, standing on the aqua carpet with bright veins in her bare feet. A girl sits cross-legged on the floor, pins in her mouth, and says, "Iv vat about vight for lengf?"

"Just right. I want only the ends of my slippers peeping out. I have stringy calves, which do not go with my pot belly." I think I'm the only one who sees Roxy as a comedian. Remember, she'd already died once. It fascinates me.

"O Miff Hunnicutt!"

Looking at Roxy, I felt a tingle of family comfort. You become a soft warm object and the brain slowly shapes itself to the facts. For a blessed moment, you are totally lacking in views.

When the little girl headed out, Roxy said she
was a bit peckish and would I be a dear and take the
Imperial and get us a couple of Big Macs? *Pour quoi
non*, I chuckled. I headed for Roosevelt Boulevard. I
never object to making a burger run. In Baby America, a fellow wants to know his fast-food inside and
out. I bought Roxy and me two mid-range burgers
and one large fries, with napkins and ketchup-paks
to go.

And Roxy sure had eyes for the little dickens,
sinking her teeth through the cheese shields with
sudden fury, cupping her left hand underneath for
drippings. Holding our hamburgers, we were both
living in the present.

She was sitting in the green silk chair, threads
poignantly snagged by cats over the years, as though
by design.

"Tracked Ruiz down."

"Oh?"

"Hand-lining grunts for Petronia Street."

"I thought so," I said.

"He had a heck of a deal here. Could've been a
sinecure. But he couldn't keep his hands off my
grapefruits."

"Seemed like there was enough to go around," I
said.

"Criminals don't think that way," said Roxy.

"No," I crooned with boredom. "I don't sup-
pose."

"Peavey and I don't plan on children."

I thought, I wonder if this is hilarious.

"Fine with me."

"He felt you might think we were going to soak

up your inheritance with babies. Have no fear. Anyway, most of it is going to that Jerry Lewis disease."

"Muscular dystrophy?"

"Yes."

"That's fine."

"Otherwise it ends up in the hands of dope peddlers, dishonest professional athletes, and corrupt disc jockeys."

"Really!"

"I think so, don't you?"

"I imagine I do."

"As to the wedding, I'll be there," she assured me.

"Me too."

"Pat wants to be maid-of-honor."

"I told him no dresses."

"I asked that you not interfere. He's having a dreadful time with his practice and there's little enough for him that brings any pleasure. Besides, she's already started by now."

"Who?"

"The seamstress, the *seamstress* who just left here."

"What about her?"

"She's fitting Pat."

"He'll never wear it. World War II and life in our family have ruined his nerve."

"Now, I am contributing to the bar three cases of my precious absinthe that Pat brought back from France when he was with Intelligence. It's for the family and you'll have to ask for it. Watch it. I have seen people get very ugly on absinthe. I have seen them be unkind to household pets and behave in every respect as though they hadn't all their buttons."

"Yes . . ."

"As you once did for a living? It's disturbing that you were in such demand."

"The theory was that I was a visionary and that I was certainly playing with a full deck."

"I'll just bet."

"Roxy, please, if you would."

"The other day your father told me he thought it was all a really good gag—"

I gave her the blankest of blank stares. Roxy stared back.

"Oh, that's right, you've decided he doesn't exist. In the father and son game, I guess that's the best stunt of all. Well, let me tell you something, you prize boob, the world is full of things that are not awaiting your description. And your father is one of them."

I felt panic.

"You and Peavey deserve each other for the aimless cruelties you commit, you evil shitsucker. I ought to kill you."

I bounded out.

When I left Roxy's, I promptly met the writer. He was looking at me and simultaneously pressing thumb and forefinger into his eyes.

"I thought you were going home," I said. I needed to know someone had one to go to.

"It's a matter of composure. It's like walking out of a bar after you've lost a fight. I'll go when I'm ready."

We strolled past La Lechonería toward the synagogue. He knew all the little streets and stared up and down with sad affection.

"I want to show you something," he said and took me down a sandy lane that passed through an open field to the sea. Even I didn't know it went to the sea. We pushed through litter and saw grass until the edge of the water; where I saw something which I took for a bad sign: six dead greyhounds rolled in the wash, eyes swollen shut with sea water.

"Losers from the track," he said. "I'm getting off the rock. I love the rock but it's a bad rock."

"Good luck."

"On what?"

"On getting shut of this place."

"Thanks. I'm going to need it."

Don and I walked downtown. Each time I go there something has changed. Today an old family jewelry store had become a moped rental drop; a small bookstore was a taco stand; and where Hart Crane and Stephen Crane had momentarily coexisted on a mildewed shelf was now an electric griddle warming a stack of pre-fab tortillas. From the gas dock I could see the flames from the Navy dump, burning at the base of a steeply leaning column of black smoke. When you sail around Fleming Key, passing downwind of the dump, the boat fills suddenly and magically with flies, millions of them, it seems, for when the fire is out, they fill the air downwind like a cloud. "You see," I said to Don. "I'm capable of noticing and remembering."

"Some things. Until you remember like you're supposed to, you're bad for the world."

"All right now, Don. You're starting to bore me. So, on your way."

"No," said Don. We were in the middle of one of those sourceless browsing mobs, the origin of my own mystery; and I wanted to move with them and feel for the moment when, on the average, they forget the highway and wherever it is they come from.

I asked Don once more to detach himself from me: it seemed that he was acquiring some suppurating need for studying me. Still, he hung on. So, right at him, in that crowd, I began to shout odd snatches from Smithsonian Institute animal records. He couldn't stand the pressure and beat a hasty retreat right up the street where I'd tried to buy that parrot. I smiled to the crowd; they soon forgot and I was once again among them, moving toward our dream of forgetfulness.

Past the Little Charles Guest House, there is a concrete house with flamingos cut in the foundations, and on that street many of the blacks speak only Spanish. There are people throwing coins against the curb and leaving the doors open on their parked cars so they can hear the radio. A couple of houses down, you can look through the lattice at the bottom, under the house, and you can see the cats all under there, kind of tortoiseshell, kind of related-looking. I began to think of the cats at the Casa Marina, in the deep grass. I began to wonder if they would be safe from the Weed Eater and those Bahamians with the grass whips.

When I went out there, the cats were arrayed against a spangle of sea light, watching the Bahamians destroy their homeland. They were in a row and rather self-possessed. It was my opinion that they would find another way of life; and the white man at the borders with the Weed Eater failed to alter that conviction.

I called Catherine at home. The little burst I'd had, feeling the cats would find a way, I wanted to spend on her.

"May I come over?"

"What can I do for you, Chet?"

"May I come over?"

"Masturbate with a crucifix?"

"I know I am a Catholic. At the same time there are other ways of viewing my conduct. I ought to strangle you."

"That's my way of saying that you have a rotten little Catholic heart, which is my privilege as a veteran of the Catholic wars, do you hear me?"

"There is no rotten little Catholic heart. There is only the Sacred Heart of Jesus and I have seen it shine in a Missouri tunic, a cane in the scabbard, on a horse named Stonewall Jackson."

"Do you know what I'm doing this very minute?"

"What?"

"I'm looking at a photograph of Jesse James in his coffin."

I slammed that phone down good. Liar, liar, liar. I know he lives.

A person I trusted at the time said it was time for me to go home, because home was a controlled environment, and that I was having a destructive effect on all and sundry out in America. It is time, he said, to leave the Sherry-Netherland and to go home; the dog is eating everything.

On the sides of the Casa Marina, there are fire escapes which are like metal stairways except that the last section is lowered from above so that the stairs can only be used going down, by someone capable of letting down that last section. Furthermore, this prevents types who might be abroad at odd hours from ascending the fire escape into the hotel. Also, on the sides of the hotel are brown ventilator exhausts which look like carp. Beyond this, I can hear the furor of my aunt's wedding from within.

On the east side, you can peer through the steel mesh at an old courtyard which lies before the sealed arches of the front of the old hotel. From here, you can barely hear the wedding. One more block and I could have lost touch entirely. I didn't have the nerve for that.

At Clarence S. Higgs Memorial Beach, I walked out the plank dock. It goes out on the water a considerable distance and then stops at the ruins of an older dock that goes another fifty yards. At this point, there is a great spoked wheel which prevents you from trying to get on the ruined dock. Turning when I got to the wheel, I was able to see the wedding crowd. I could see that boat too. And Jorge Cruz's orchestra sent its strains of Old Key West across this new seascape where pilings sucked in the tide like regret. It was time to start for the wedding.

I turned into the hotel by the old octagonal lounge, whose weird acoustics had put the bar out of business. The wedding was still not in sight but Catherine was waiting for me. She was wearing a silk dress with angular shoulders, like Billie Holiday; and she had a red flower in her hair. She was wearing about a half of a coffee can of old jewelry and carrying a little beaded purse in both hands. When I looked at her, I fell in love all over again. At the same time, it was like watching something through a window. My heart had lost its purchase, its ability to do anything for anyone, and could only register. But it had perhaps never registered more.

"How is the wedding?" I asked.

"Very well. They all are taking it very seriously. Roxy has her man and Peavey has his waterfront."

"God, Catherine. I miss my old show. It was like this in many ways."

"I thought about their marriage. It's fair. Let's go in and dance."

We walked into the old homeland of the cats. There was a small crowd among the abandoned buildings. The swimming pool was empty and on the concrete ramp for the long-gone diving boards I thought I glimpsed a familiar figure and that he was staring at me.

I watched the wedding as closely as I could. There was the turmoil of the party behind which the slower geometry of ceremony could be seen, to the extent that I *would* see, knowing what a meat cleaver daily history is and how we trend, despite our most luminous acts, steadily toward oblivion. Whether I refused to look or refused to remember just didn't matter any more. For me, viewing the perpetual stream of leftovers, I could only conclude once more that the dog ate the part we didn't like. I had the only reasonable motive in the place: I wanted to dance.

I took Catherine in my arms. I thought the orchestra was playing the same song I'd heard from the dock. They were dressed in yellowing linen. There were many people dancing and I cast my eyes about blindly, avoiding, for the moment, any recognition while my beloved and I danced at the edge of the sea.

My uncle Pat soared past, wearing one of his twenty-year-old seersucker suits. I knew that the dress would hang reproachfully in his closet forever. I winked over Catherine's shoulder and he winked back. He knew that I knew.

Nylon Pinder wore white shoes and pants with a white patent-leather belt secured by a Wells Fargo replica buckle. He sported a polyester nik-nik shirt with pastel clouds and the faces of women of the 1930's superimposed on flying borzois. Nylon was hugely moved by the ceremony. He shook my hand with both of his and said simply: "It is the dawn of a great era." The morning paper had spattered his tongue with new phrases. Nevertheless, he still bore the livid scar on his cheek, one further mark of the all-consuming dog.

Catherine had put her head on my shoulder as we danced. When Roxy and Peavey came into our view, I asked if we could double-cut, and we did.

"Well, I've done it," said Roxy.

"My congratulations."

"I think you will agree the end is always in sight."

"The end of what?"

"The end of the absinthe."

"Is that what you meant?"

She said, "No."

I guess Catherine and I had danced a half hour or so when I first spotted Marcelline with her boyfriend. I might have seen them earlier but I was not looking in the direction of the diving board; and I believe the two of them had been lurking in the sea grapes over there.

The boyfriend wore a sparkling Hawaiian shirt and Marcelline had, once more, her air of corrupt glamour, bits of bright string and ribbon tied in her hair, blatant paste rings on every finger.

"Your family have been here a long time, haven't they?" asked the boyfriend indulgently.

"Yes, yes they have."

"Isn't that your father?"

"No," I said.

"How up are you on local history?"

"Not that up."

"You ever heard about Lieutenant Pomeroy?"

"I don't think so."

Our dancing came to a complete stop. Marcelline put her hand in my back pocket.

"Well," said the boyfriend, "he was a native of Key West who fought the pirates two hundred years ago." They were leading us toward the sea grapes. "He was killed escorting a slave ship from Havana." We were in the trees at the edge of the sea now. I could hear hermit crabs in the awkward roots where the tide glided unmercifully. "He might have been kin to you."

"Why are you telling me about Lieutenant Pomeroy?"

"Well uh, Marcelline and I are kind of low, kind of cash-poor right now—"

"And what?" Dread arose. The boyfriend picked up the sack from between the roots.

"Do you want to buy him?"

He stretched open the sack and there was Lieutenant Pomeroy.

Marcelline said, "It's purely historical. I mean, there's no jewelry. There's some military buttons and a sword handle. But we guarantee he's complete."

I glimpsed the bones glowing in the sack and turned suddenly. "No," I said. Catherine was already gone. I hurried to the dancers and still I couldn't see her. Then, from nowhere, she passed close to me, carrying her wrap.

"It was awful," I said, aching with hope and guilt.

"You attract that sort of thing like a lightning rod."

"*I do not!*" I said desperately. I could see it coming.

"Then why why why do these things always happen to us?"

"Oh please, darling, don't blame me for it. I didn't do it."

"Sweetie, I can't stand it."

And then she was gone. I watched her in her silk dress go shimmering through the palms and vanish. Then a bright car filled the space she'd gone through and spilled dancers onto the lawn.

When I turned around, he was walking from the diving board toward me. Roxy and Peavey stood amid applause and elevated glasses. He said, "This is a sham but it's not my money. I'll see you at your place at twelve. No sense staying beyond that."

By the time I got to Catherine's, there was a cab in front and suitcases on the sidewalk. There were bones all over the yard.

"Is that Lieutenant Pomeroy?" I asked.

"Yes, they said they'd have never gone and gotten him if we were going to take it like that. They said we made them feel like second-class citizens."

"Going to the bus?"

"Yes, I am."

"Can I ride over with you?"

"Sure."

"Aren't you going to change?"

She was wearing her wedding clothes.

"No."

"Can we make love one last time?"

"No."

"Is there anything I can do?"

"There's nothing in the house I want. Marcelline and that guy took the stereo in exchange for the skeleton. They were blown out and I was afraid to argue with them."

We got the suitcases into the cab and sat in the back. When tears first came, the red flower in Catherine's hair blurred until it filled the air. Then I stopped.

"Where are you going?" I asked.

"Thinking of going to Panama."

"Why?"

"It's the last place I saw you." She pressed her beautiful hands to her face and said, "In Panama I'm married. I have a man and he'll stand up for me through th•ick and thin. Everywhere else I'm in pieces."

I will say for myself, when it all comes rattling down, that I bought her ticket to the mainland. She said, "You can die trying." And the hydraulic doors closed behind her before I could tell her it was still the best way to go. When the bus swung around I saw the red flower in the window; and because I thought our souls would be together forever, I believed it was the third window from the left. I knew I would never see Catherine again.

At twelve o'clock Jesse came, a cane in the scabbard, his years at sea, the difficulties with the smokey subways of Boston behind him. He said, "We want the same thing." He stepped through the door as though he owned the place and asked what I called him Jesse for. I told him you have so many names for things that matter. He walked across the room, leaned down, and turned on the lamp. Then he cut his eyes straight up to his portrait on the wall.

"When was that taken?" he asked.

"Ten years ago."

"I'm wearing out fast," he said and reached his hands out in front of himself. He gazed at their age spots. "I never thought I'd look like this."

"Well, you do." I sat down.

"You know who I am," he said quietly. "Can't you say hello?"

When I was young, we used to dive into the swimming pool from the highest board on moonless nights, without looking to see if there was water in the pool, knowing that it was emptied twice a month. I felt the same blind arc through darkness when I spoke to my father. He just watched me say the word and after that either of us could go, knowing there was more to be said and time to say it. Perhaps we wished there was not so much time.